Till Death Do Us Part

DC Caruso

Radiant Publishing House Inc.
P.O. Box 379
Walden, NY 12586
www.radiantpublishinghouse.com

Paperback
ISBN-13: 978-1-953682-00-0

Dedication Page

To Mama and Dad—for always being proud of me and giving me my guiding light -xoxo Daughter #1.

Till Death Do Us Part

Acknowledgments

Dearest Concetta Guido,
You truly are one of the nicest people I have ever met. You are an extraordinarily great editor, and I have loved working with you. You flawlessly fluffed my story in all the right places and took it from flat to fabulous. I thank you from the bottom of my heart. Bam! X0

Michael, where do I begin...
Thank you for introducing me to RPH and making me a part of it. Thank you for always spreading positivity in my life and in my writing. Thank you for always pushing me a little harder so that I can fearlessly reach my fullest potential. Thank you for always having my back. Thank you for all you are and all you do for me. X0X0

Till Death Do Us Part

DC Caruso

Table of Contents

Till Death Do Us Part

Dear Reader,

In your hands is a tale of fight, courage, loss, and love. Contained within these pages, you'll discover a ransoming energy that will keep you turning this relatable plot twister until the very last sentence.

I should know—I've had the sincerest pleasure of working closely with DC Caruso on it. And that was exactly my reaction. The author has created captivating characters set in a very modern story.

If you don't believe me, read it for yourself, you won't regret it.

Till Death Do Us Part honors the values and sanctity of marriage, the exciting and thrilling ride of first love in all of its forms, and how those meant to find you—will—when you least expect it.

Dear Reader, I can say, without a doubt—that this is the most fun I've had with a romance novel, ever.

Happy reading, and all the best!

Concetta Guido

Executive Editor

Till Death Do Us Part

~Chapter 1~

The Funeral

All is quiet in St. Charles Cemetery, as it should be. I am standing next to Father Layhe, on the side of Nate's coffin as he speaks about my brother. I never thought he would be the first to go. He was younger than I, healthier, and so much stronger.

How could this happen? I ask myself this question repeatedly, every day since he passed. The doctors believed that he had a heart attack behind the wheel of his car when he was driving home from work. They feel this must have caused him to lose control of his car and crash it into the tree. The saying goes that most accidents happen within five minutes of your home. In this case, that was very true.

His girlfriend is standing at the head of his coffin, pretending to be completely devastated as she hunches over in her accentuating fitted black dress, falsely sobbing into a tissue. I never liked her, she is too much of a phony, and I can see right through her—starting with her platinum blonde hair. I always asked him what he saw in her and his reply would be, "she's great in bed." And with that, we would both laugh hysterically.

One day before he passed, he revealed what it really was that he saw in her. He saw a decent person in her, on top of being incredibly attractive. He also revealed that he felt he could not do any better. Nate was never very good at choosing a mate. My brother usually hung out in bars and picked up whoever looked good to him after he had several drinks in him. I told him he went about it all the wrong way.

With today's technology and all the dating websites out there, I felt he had a better chance of finding a better woman suited for him if he gave one of those a try. Match.com is a popular site, and I have several friends who found their perfect mate on there and married them, too. As close as we were, he never listened to me, told me that he's old-fashioned, and did not want to turn to the internet to find the woman of his dreams.

"Emma? Are you okay, dear?" Asked Father Layhe.

I snapped out of my thoughts and answered quickly, "Umm, yes, Father. I'm okay."

"Would you like to speak now, on behalf of your brother?"

"Yes, I would. Thank you, Father. As you all know, Nate and I were remarkably close. We did everything together; went to the same college, hung out with the same friends, and worked our first job at the same supermarket. I adored him, and if we could ask him how he felt about me, I am sure he would say I was his *Pipsqueak.* He was a great guy, the kind of guy that would do anything for anyone. His sudden passing is devastating to me, and he will always be on my mind and in my heart. I love you, Nate. Rest easy till we meet again," I said as a loud sob caught in my throat.

It was so hard to hold it all together as I said this, and the tears streamed uncontrollably down my face. I glanced up to look at Leah, who did not even shed a tear throughout my eulogy, only to see her talking and smiling at one of my brother's best friends. She confirmed what I always said to Nate, that she is one big *phony!*

When she caught me looking, she took a tissue from her purse and wiped at her eyes.

Yeah, okay! I am sure this was for my eyes only. For all I know, she was planning to hook up with Caden, Nate's best friend later.

Is he seeing this now from up above? I can only hope.

Father Layhe finished his sermon, hugged me tightly, and a couple of Nate's friends, as well. He then made his way through the crowd to a car that was waiting for him. I thanked everyone for coming and stayed behind. I felt like I needed some time alone with my brother. There was so much more I needed to say to him and asked the cemetery worker to please give me more time, and to come back later to lower him into the ground.

I stood next to his shiny white coffin with my hand resting at the head of it while I spoke out loud to him, "Nate, I'm missing you like crazy right now, and I need you to know that I will forever love you and hold you close in my heart. How will I ever go on without you? You were my best friend, my confidant, and my protector. My life will be so empty now."

I was running out of time. I continued talking for a couple of hours until the administrator from the cemetery office came up to me, explained that the cemetery was closing now and that I had to leave. I wanted to beg for just five more minutes, but I knew that it would not matter. It was all over now. Nate was gone, and I was alone.

After I entered my car, I cried. I cried harder than I think I ever had in my life. I was startled when a man knocked on my driver's window. I rolled down the window just a bit to hear what he was saying. I was greeted by a pair of softened piercing blue eyes that bore into me.

"Miss, are you okay? Do you want me to call someone for you?" He asked kindly.

"Yes, umm, no… I mean, I will be okay. Thank you so much," I said as I rolled up my window, wiped my eyes, and started my car. It was getting dark out and I needed to get home. I had an anxious puppy waiting to eat and be walked.

I could not help but think about Nate on the drive. I found myself talking out loud to him as if it would make him appear here again with me. I was not ready to let him go. I do not think I would ever be ready for that.

"Death is so final. Why do people have to die?" I spoke into the air as I drove.

Life is just not fair.

I pulled up into my driveway in the front of my house to see a car I did not recognize. As I got out of my car, the guy, Nate's best friend who was talking to Leah, got out of his. I had known Caden throughout my high school years as he and Nate grew closer. Caden was almost always around, and we teased one another frequently. Borderline flirting. And maybe it was a little cliche, crushing on my brother's best friend. But out of respect for Nate, nothing had ever happened. Still, I trusted him. At the very least, I thought we had an understanding between us. This was a behavior I hardly expected from someone that both Nate and I had thought was loyal.

"Hi, Em, I just wanted to make sure you were okay. I know how close you two were, and I just felt like I needed to check in on you," he said.

I would have been much happier to see you if you weren't just cozying up to my brother's skanky ex.

"Okay, thanks. I'm sure Nate would be happy you checked in on me. I did see you talking to Leah, though. You both looked a little chummy at my brother's funeral. It looked quite inappropriate to me. She was smiling and acting all flirty with you, and my brother wasn't even in the ground just yet! A bit rude, don't you think?" I spat out angrily at him.

His eyes expanded to nearly twice their size as I called him out. *Caught? Or mortified? I was committed to the anger I was feeling. I was just so...disappointed in him!*

"Wait, Em, it's not what it looks like. We umm… we weren't being chummy." Caden's cocoa-brown eyes could hardly meet mine. Nervously, he swept his hand back through his shaggy dirty-blonde locks, resting just at the nape of his neck. "She had some news that she wanted to tell me." He shifted uncomfortably from one foot to the other, where I could see the tears in his blue jeans exposing a hint of his thigh.

I hardly had the patience for how handsome he looked. If there was ever a time I had felt something for Caden, that was a fleeting moment. Lost now to time and memories. "Listen, Caden, I really don't want to hear what she had to say. I just buried my brother. I'm sorry, I have to go." I turned on my heel and walked quickly into my house, slamming the door behind me.

All I could think of was how Caden had no clue! My brother just died, and he is trying to get with Leah. What is wrong with him? He really could not have been much of a best friend if this is what he is doing! *Ugh, I have such a migraine!*

As soon as I walked into the house, Boomer came running up to me with his tail wagging. Somehow, that made things a little better. I remember the day we went to get him. Nate suggested that we should go to *Man's Best Friend,* the rescue shelter in town. He said he was sure I would fall in love with a pup there. And he was so right! When we walked in, we were greeted by this black lab pup that was just so cute and friendly. He was only six months old and had huge paws. We were told his previous owner turned him in because they felt he was too high energy for them. *How dumb.*

Didn't they do their research first? Labs are a bit high energy, sure, but if you let them run around, they burn it off. He's so beautiful; he has that adorable square head and a super shiny black coat. I guess you can say it was love at first sight. There were times when Nate used to say that *I* hadn't picked *him*, rather *Boomer* had picked *me,* and I chuckled at the thought. Boomer loved Nate, too. Nate came to my house quite a bit to take Boomer on walks and to play with him. I know Boomer will be missing Nate, as well.

I fed and walked Boomer, and I even tried to play with him a bit. But I am so sad, that my heart is just not in it. I swear that he can sense how I feel. He keeps licking my face and standing right by my side. They say dogs have emotions and feelings too, and I strongly believe that.

I could not help but run today's events through my head. Seeing Leah talking to Caden, whispering in his ear, and them laughing about whatever she was saying. That was so hurtful and in such poor taste. How could they do that? She was his girlfriend, and he was his best friend. I do not think I can ever forgive either one of them for that behavior.

It was getting late, and if I did not stop thinking about these things, I would never fall asleep. As I undressed and turned to the full-length mirror in my bedroom, my mind began to overprocess. It was bad enough that I was worried about the fact that Nate possibly died of a heart attack before he crashed his car into the tree.

Nate and I shared similar features from the dark hair that we got from our mother. He was only thirty-eight and had gained some weight over the years. We both had. He was just a little overweight, and I am sure that could have contributed to his health. But here I am—a lot more overweight than he was, so this scares me even more.

When I get up tomorrow, I seriously need to think about dieting and getting into shape. The fact that I sit for a living does not help me. I am sure it adds to my weight problem.

"Come on, Boomer, let's go to bed."

As if he understood exactly what I said, he ran ahead of me up the stairs and jumped right into my bed. I climbed in next to him and reached into the first drawer to my nightstand and withdrew the journal Nate had gifted me for my birthday last year. Up until now, I had never had a desire to use it, and I have heard that journaling is really good for us in terms of helping to keep our emotions in check.

So, if I'm to focus on my health, this is a pretty good first start.

After writing a brief entry and jotting my feelings out, I wrapped my arms around Boomer's hairy body, and closed my eyes. This has been the longest, most horrible day of my life. Tomorrow will be a new beginning. For me, and for Nate.

"Good night, Nate, I love you," I said out loud as I stared at the ceiling and finally fell asleep from sheer exhaustion.

Damn it, Journal!

Why? Why? WHY?! I just want to scream! Why did God take Nate from me? How could He? I thought I was a good and kind person, who always put herself last.

So why was Nate taken from me? What have I done to be punished? I don't understand. I want to.

I'm just so...I can't find the words, Journal. I'm lost for them, as I'm lost without my best friend.

How are Boomer and I going to move on without him?

I hope I can figure it out soon.

~Emma

Till Death Do Us Part

~Chapter 2~

The Newspaper Ad

Like I told Nate last night, today I am going to start eating right and be healthier. While watching the news this morning, I saw a commercial for Weight Watchers and I decided that I'd give it a try. I downloaded the app and I called the 800-phone number to ask some questions I had about getting started. The representative on the phone was genuinely nice and highly informative. I felt I could do this, and it wouldn't be too difficult. What I mostly had to do was add some sort of physical activity to my daily routine. Since Nate would not be here anymore to take Boomer for his walks, I figured that I would start with that.

"Come Boomer; want to go for a walk?"

Almost immediately, he stopped bathing himself, jumped up, and ran to the front door. I know how much he used to love his walks with Nate. I hope he has just as much fun with me too.

I grabbed my keys, shut my door, and off we went. It was as if Boomer was leading the way. He walked straight down the block to the corner, turned left, and continued down the path. I had no idea where we were going at first, but Boomer seemed to know exactly where he was going.

To my surprise, we ended up right at the cemetery. How did he know? They say that animals, especially dogs, can be very perceptive. But I had just buried Nate yesterday, and Boomer had not been to the cemetery yet.

It was even more perplexing when Boomer led me right to Nate's grave. And then he did something that made my heart ache further. He laid down on Nate's grave as if he were laying across his body like he did so many times when Nate would lay on the floor and play with him. Boomer put his head down on the dirt at the head of the grave and let out a long sigh. I watched him closely as a tear escaped his eye, rolled down his face, and left a moist streak down to the tip of his nose. With that, I lost it and started hysterically crying all over again. How were Boomer and I ever going to live without Nate?

He was everything to us.

There was a loud crunching of leaves behind me and I looked up to see a familiar face. It was the man who knocked on my window last night when I had just gotten into my car. He was on one knee bending down over another grave with a very large tombstone. I did not want to stare, but I made a mental note of curiosity to read the tombstone when we left.

Boomer laid on Nate's grave a little longer as I silently said a couple of prayers and talked to Nate. I looked up at the sky and asked my brother to give me a sign that he knew Boomer and I were here with him. A few moments later, one cloud appeared in the sky. One—and only one— cloud appeared right above us. Tears streamed from my eyes because I knew in my heart, it was Nate. He always told me he would *move heaven and earth for me* if he could. And now, he did all he could to move a cloud.

It was heaven he was moving for me.

"I love and miss you so much Nate, and so does Boomer. Thank you for moving heaven for me, I'd move Earth for you!" I shouted out loud into the air, not giving a damn who heard me. I did not care if the man behind me did, either. I turned to look at him, and he had a sympathetic smile on his face as he waved. I raised my hand as if to say, *I'm sorry.*

I picked up Boomer's leash and decided it was time to head back home. It felt good to take a walk, and I felt like this should be a daily circuit for me with Boomer. We will make the cemetery our destination. I needed the exercise, and so did Boomer.

"Goodbye, Nate. Boomer and I will see you tomorrow. I love you! Boomer does, too." As I said this, Boomer barked as if he agreed.

We strolled by the tombstone that the man was kneeling in front of. I assumed that the grave belonged to his wife. The tombstone stated, *"Beloved wife, and daughter…"* and he put fresh flowers on her grave. The flowers were a lovely fall bouquet with an array of several different colors. They complimented the floral design on the tombstone nicely.

Boomer and I picked up the pace because the sky was getting dark and the forecast called for rain today mixed with thunderstorms.

When we got home, I saw Caden's car in my driveway again. As soon as we approached the driveway, he jumped out of the car. Boomer started barking wildly because he did not know him. Caden stopped dead in his tracks and didn't come any closer.

Caden held his hands up and out to show he came in peace. "Hi, Em, I am so sorry to bother you. I really need to talk to you. Before you say anything, I wanted to tell you something I think you should know. Can we talk?"

I looked down at Boomer, who seemed to take care of my lack of desire to see my brother's best friend. Gently, I patted him. "Caden, I really don't see what there is left to say. I need to get Boomer in the house, and I have things I need to do."

Though, he was persistent. He wasn't giving in so soon, a trait that sometimes grated Nate's nerves. Now, it was grating mine. "Emma, please! Leah's pregnant with Nate's baby!" Caden blurted out suddenly.

"What? How do you know this? Are you *sure* it's Nate's baby?" I asked.

Slowly, he lowered his hands. "Yes, I'm positive. When we were at the cemetery for Nate's funeral, she whispered it into my ear. That's when you saw her smile and laugh," he explained.

"Oh my God!" I gasped. "What is she going to do?"

"She said she is going to keep the baby and raise it on her own. She said Nate would want her to do this."

"Wow, okay... I don't know what to say."

"Em, I just felt you would want to know. She does not intend to try to find you to tell you. I know you two only met a couple of times, and that you were not too fond of her. Frankly, neither was I. I tried to tell you this last night, but you assumed I was trying to get with her. And you seemed angry with me. I'm sorry my timing was so off, but I felt that you should know as soon as possible," said Caden.

"Thank you. And I'm so sorry, Caden. I just thought your intentions were somewhat off-key. How pregnant is she?"

"She's five and a half months pregnant, and the doctor said she's carrying very small. He also said the baby will grow more rapidly as the pregnancy progresses," explained Caden.

"Did Nate know?"

"Yes, he was planning on meeting you for dinner that night to tell you. He was so happy."

"Caden, I have to go. It's starting to rain. Thank you and take care."

"Em, be well. Here's my cell number if you ever need anything," said Caden as he handed me his business card. "I'm leaving for Milan on business in a couple of days. So, let me know before I go. You could always use my number while I'm away, too."

"Thanks. How long will you be away?"

"For a year or two. I won't know till I'm there for at least six months."

"Okay, thanks again. Safe travels," I said and turned around without looking back.

Caden took me totally by surprise with the news he had to share. All I could think about was this baby now, and that I wanted *and* needed to be a part of its life. But how? I really had no idea what I was going to do.

I had taken off from work to mourn my brother and had a week to myself. I thought I would concentrate on my diet, exercise plan, and job hunt for a part-time job. I currently work from home as a virtual assistant for a friend who lives in Florida.

I am also writing a book about the paranormal. For years I have had paranormal things happen to me, so I decided to write a book in my spare time. I love writing, I always did, but all of my short stories that have been printed have not brought in a lot of money. So, for now, my writing is just more like a hobby until I hit it big by writing *The Great American Novel*. I laughed out loud despite myself, and Boomer joined in by jumping on me and barking.

Looking back, I remember one day I was sitting on my couch watching TV when suddenly the candles on my coffee table relit themselves! It scared me half to death. I had blown them out just before I got up to get my dinner, as I did not want to smell the scent while I was eating.

Then last Christmas, I had some friends over for dinner and we were eating in the kitchen, when we heard a loud crash in the living room. We all jumped up to see what happened. The first thing we noticed was that my Christmas tree was laying on the floor, and many of my glass ornaments were smashed. Then, I noticed that my stockings were pulled from my fireplace and thrown on the couch. I still do not know what happened that night. I did not have Boomer, so I couldn't blame him. I know it was the work of an angry person. I could feel that when I entered the room. The air was so thick I could slice through it with a knife.

I grabbed the paper off the front porch and sat down with a cup of peppermint tea. I did not feel like eating much right now and the peppermint would soothe my stomach. I went straight to the *Help Wanted* section. I saw an ad that caught my eye:

> *Nanny needed FT for an Infant.*
>
> *Job to commence in 6 months.*
>
> *Call Leah Morris: 570-555-1214.*

I could not believe my eyes! Was this the same Leah, my brother's ex-girlfriend? Could it really be? I know who would have the answer to that.

I pulled out the card Caden gave me. I grabbed my cell phone and texted him.

"Caden, is Leah's last name Morris?" I asked him.

"Yes. I assume you saw the ad in today's paper?" He texted back almost immediately.

"Yeah. Okay, thanks."

"Sure," Caden replied.

I decided to text Leah. I figured the only way I was going to see Nate's baby when he or she was born and get to watch the baby grow would be if I became the nanny Leah was looking for. Crazy idea, I know, but it was so important for me to know his child. This is the only way I could think of making it happen.

"Hello, Leah. I would like to inquire about how I can apply for the job as a nanny for your infant," I texted nervously.

"You can give me your email address, and I will send you an informal application."

"Thank you, my email is iwrite103@gmail.com. I will fill it out as soon as I get it, and send it right back to you."

"Great. I look forward to reviewing it." Was Leah's last text.

I put my phone down and my heart and mind started racing!

What had I just done? Am I crazy?

"Nate, you're going to have a baby in just a few months! I hope you can hear me. You need to be a part of your baby's life however you can. God bless you and the baby. I hope it's a girl!" I yelled out into the air.

I was no longer nervous. I think my nervousness just turned into excitement. Nate was going to have a baby! I needed to start crocheting a blanket for the baby, too. No matter what, I was going to be a huge part of its life. I will go to whatever extent that I must. God help me!

I printed out the application and looked at it. It was actually very simplistic. Just a few obvious questions: name, address, cell number, references, experience, etc. I took my time filling it out. I was confident that Leah wouldn't know that it was me. She didn't know my last name, for starters. All she knew was that I was Nate's sister. Nate and I had different last names, too. His last name was Wilcox, and mine was Porter. We had the same mom but different dads.

I guess my plan was to apply for the job and not tell her who I was. She didn't like me very much, either. I am guessing it was because of the close relationship that Nate and I shared. Nate always put me first and sometimes that meant that his *girl of the hour* had to wait. And Leah is the most impatient person I have ever met. Nate used to tell me that when he was on the phone with me or someone else and she was in the room, she would pace back and forth clearly showing she was agitated. She wanted his attention twenty-four-seven. *So immature of her,* if you ask me.

The only problem I could foresee would be that when I showed up for the interview, she would see it was me. And she would not give me the job.

Dear Journal,

As luck would have it, I saw that Leah placed an ad in the newspaper for a nanny for her baby, Nate's baby! I must be crazy, but I applied for the job. I pray Leah doesn't recognize me. Maybe I should change my appearance to ensure she doesn't know it's me.

But how…?

I am just so excited; I feel this will guarantee that I will be a big part of Nate's baby's life. Fingers crossed, wish me luck Journal!

~Emma

~Chapter 3~

The Date

I sent back the application. Her response was quick and favorable. She said she felt I was a good fit for the position as Nanny for her baby. She explained that she would be doing interviews as it got closer to her due date. Leah also finished up by saying I was her first choice, so far. I said a little prayer to Nate, and to God, that I would win out in the end and get this job to help raise my niece or nephew. I know Nate would want it this way.

I had a date tonight for the first time in a long while. I really did not feel like going; however, I thought it might create a good diversion. I know Nate would want me to get on with my life, so I decided not to cancel the date.

There was a new Italian restaurant that just opened up on the corner of Main and Maple. *Donato's Italian Restaurant* was written up in our town paper and had several 5-star reviews from customers that dined there. So, when Adam, my date, suggested we try there, I jumped at the opportunity. Fingers crossed it's as good as the reviews say.

Today is Friday, *errand day,* as I like to call it. It's also my payday. I decided to complete things on my list in reverse. I usually follow my to-do list in the order I write things down. But I sometimes feel I can be a bit OCD, so I decided to switch it up. I was going to go to the nail salon last, but now I will make this my first stop. Suzie, my manicurist, is a single mom of one daughter and is a real sweetheart. She also gives a great hand massage.

"Hey, Suzie! I was wondering if you could take me now for a manicure, instead of at my regular appointment at 2 pm." I asked.

Suzie turned to face me as her thickly mascaraed brown eyes lit up, her ruby lips parted excitedly as her southern drawl exclaimed, "Emma! I am so happy to see ya! I'm so sorry about Nate; I know how close you two were."

"Thanks so much, Suzie. It's been really hard. But I know Nate is with me now, and he'll always be in my heart."

"Yes, he will darlin'. Now go pick yourself a color and take a seat at my station."

I decided to pick a navy-blue color, in honor of Nate. Blue was his favorite color. Any shade of blue, actually. I might just sport a different shade of blue every two weeks for a few months. As I thought of him, I just wanted to scream, *how Nate? How could this have happened?* I tried hard to stifle the urge to cry again.

Just then, Suzie popped her head around the corner, her long red acrylics tapped against the wall. I could now see her paisley skirt that drifted past her knee with a hint of her favorite worn cowboy boot. "Hey, girl. Miss me?" She laughed.

"You know it, Sista," I answered as I wiped a tear from my eye.

"Aww, don't shed them tears no more. Y'all know that brother of yours wouldn't want ya to."

I clutched the bottle of nail polish in my hand. "Yes, I know. You are so right. I just keep trying to picture my life without him. And I'm trying so hard to move on, but it still hurts."

Suzie tilted her head sympathetically as she reached to put a hand on my shoulder. "I know, sweetie. Listen, you're still going on a date with that guy you met at the *Pork & Rind*?"

"Yes, the date's tonight. Why?"

"I just wanna make sure. You deserve that. You go have yourself a grand ol' time. And no thinkin' about Nate, now. Ya hear?"

"Yes," I laughed, knowing she was right.

Suzie finished up polishing my nails, she picked up my purse, my cell phone, and led the way to the nail dryers. After she put my stuff down and turned on the dryers, she hugged me tightly.

"Now listen, girl, you have fun on that date, and I wanna hear all about it in two weeks when y'all come back to see me. Ya hear?"

"You're the best, Suzie! What would I do without you?"

"Well, let's see, you ain't ever gonna know, sweetie; because, I'm not goin' anywheres!"

"Thanks, hon," I said as I leaned into her.

Suzie really is an amazing woman. She became pregnant with her daughter when she was just eighteen years old and graduating from high school. Her boyfriend at the time wanted nothing to do with her if she was going to keep the baby. She told him she could not—and would not—ever give up her baby. So, as expected, he left her.

She continued to waitress at night while her mom watched her baby. At the same time, she went to Beauty School to pursue her career in Cosmetology. When she graduated, she went to a local salon, applied for a job, and was hired immediately. The owner of the shop was in her 70s. She was ill and did not know how much longer she had left on this earth.

One day, she came to Suzie and asked her if she would want to purchase the salon. Suzie said she would love to, but that she did not have any money to give her for it. The salon owner worked out a plan so that a small portion of Suzie's weekly income would go towards purchasing the salon. And in the event of the owner's death, that Suzie would inherit the business. The attorney drew up the papers and they both signed them. Martha, the previous owner of the salon died less than a year later. Suzie was forever grateful for the gift of the salon. She tries to give back to the community, in Martha's name, as often as she can. Suzie is one special person. So was Martha, I suppose.

When I left the salon, I glanced at my list and I decided my next stop would be to go get that pretty blouse I saw at the mall a little while back. It would go perfectly with the gray and black plaid slacks I planned on wearing on the date. But first, I need to grab something light to eat. I was starving. I forgot I had not eaten anything this morning. All I drank was tea.

I needed to stay within my dietary constraints, so I chose the salad bar in the food court. I piled on the lettuce, and then the broccoli. From there, I added some chopped walnuts, red peppers, and onions. I opted for a light vinaigrette dressing. I didn't see any fat free dressings.

Then, I grabbed a bottle of water and headed towards the cashier.

"That'll be $12.69, ma'am," said the young boy behind the register.

"Thank you," I said as I handed him my debit card.

Wow, I thought to myself, *that was a lot of money for a salad.* I probably could have made the same thing for a third of the price. But then again, this was the mall. I feel like everything is overpriced here, anyways.

I sat down near the entrance into the food court. There was one that was available up front. As I was eating, I glanced up to see the same man that I have been seeing everywhere lately. It was so strange! I saw him at the cemetery where I buried Nate, then I saw him there again when I was there with Boomer, and now here.

Coincidence? Or the work of Nate Wilcox from above? Hmm...

As he walked past my table, I glanced up and he smiled. He had a dazzling smile, actually, for being an older man. His teeth were perfectly straight and very white; his eyes were bright blue, and contrasted well with his salt and pepper hair. This mysterious stranger was dressed nicely, as well. He had on newer looking jeans and a dark gray dress shirt with the sleeves cuffed up.

I finished eating and walked back past him to throw my garbage away. I smiled back at him. He looked like he was going to say something, but I just buzzed right by him and did not acknowledge it. I had to get home and get ready for my date. I was not in the mood to engage in conversation with him, anyway.

When I arrived home, Boomer was barking up a storm. I had no idea what was wrong.

"Boomer, what's up, boy?" I asked as though he could answer me.

Boomer ran to the back door and I could see that someone had tried to break in! *Oh my God!* I grabbed Boomer, got into my car, and called the police. I was not going to continue to stay in my house just in case the intruder was still around.

"9-1-1 What's your emergency?"

"I came home, my dog was barking, and I think someone was trying to get in my house or they may be still on my property!" I said excitedly.

"Okay, ma'am, where are you now?"

"I took my dog and I'm sitting in my car in the driveway." I was shaking, as I said it.

"Ma'am, pull out of your driveway and down the road a bit where you can still see your home. I want you out of harm's way. What is your address?" said the 911 dispatcher.

"It's 731 Oak Drive," I said, as I pulled out of the driveway. "I'm two houses down, and I can still see my home very clearly from here."

"Okay, great. I have dispatched the police, and they will be there in three to five minutes. Stay where you are and watch the house. When you see the police arrive, you may drive up to your home and get out of the car to identify yourself."

"Okay, thank you," I said as I hung up the phone.

I sat in my car shaking like a leaf. I was trying to rationalize what just happened. I know Boomer would protect the house and I, but he's no match for a crazy person or someone with a gun. And God forbid something happened to Boomer, I could not be without him, too!

I saw the police car pull up and come to a screeching halt, then two others. One was an unmarked car. I drove up closer to my house and parked in front. I got out and left Boomer in the car with the windows open a little bit. I pressed the lock on the remote while I was walking over to the police.

"Hi, I'm Emma Porter. This is my house," I said.

"Hi, Emma, I'm Detective Johnson, and this is Officer Parsons. I just sent in two officers to check your home. They said it was all clear. No one was in the house. Now, tell me exactly what happened."

"I came home, and I pulled into my driveway. I could hear Boomer, my dog, barking, and going wild. When I walked in, Boomer did not come running like he usually does. He was staring and barking at my back door. As I got closer to the door, I noticed the lock was busted and the door was slightly ajar. There were black dirty handprints on the inside of the white door where the lock is. That's when I grabbed Boomer and put him in the car and called 9-1-1."

"Hey, Johnson, what do we have here?" Asked a man with a rich, deep, and authoritative voice.

I turned around to see who he was talking to and I was shocked to see it was *him*!

"It's *you!*" I said in surprise.

"It's *you*, too!" Laughed the mysterious stranger.

"Umm, you guys know each other or something?" Asked Johnson.

"Kind of. Hi, I'm Lieutenant Owens, and you are?" He asked as he extended his hand for me to shake.

I was unable to hide my awe, "I'm Emma Porter. Nice to meet you, sir."

I couldn't believe my eyes. This was so weird! This guy keeps showing up everywhere I go. What are the chances of that?

"Okay, the house is secure so you guys can go. Johnson, just go back to the station, write up the report and give me a copy. I'll get it to Ms. Porter later," said Lieutenant Owens.

"Ms. Porter, pull your car in the driveway and I'll meet you at your front door and walk you in."

"I will. Thank you," I said.

I walked quickly back to the car. Boomer was panting hard and probably needed water. I pet his head and then drove into the driveway. I put on Boomer's leash and took him out of the car. I saw the Lieutenant waiting on my porch.

When I approached him, he reached out to pet Boomer's head. Boomer seemed to take a liking to him. They always say if your dog likes and trusts someone, then you can trust them, too. So, I'm going with Boomer's instincts on this one.

He held the door for Boomer and I, and we all walked in. I asked the handsome lieutenant if he would like a cup of tea. He said he would, but that he wanted to secure my backdoor first to ensure no one would be able to come in. He suggested I call an alarm company and get an alarm with cameras installed as soon as possible.

He fixed the door while I was calling a locksmith to change the locks. Then, my next call was going to be to the alarm company that my neighbors use. The Smiths have a sign on their front lawn that has the name *Safeguard* on it and the phone number.

Owens sat down at the island in my kitchen. He sipped his oolong tea while his eyes followed me, those piercing blues encasing me, looking right through me. I'm guessing that in his line of work he needs to size a person up to form an opinion about them.

"Why do you think someone would try to break into your house?" He asked.

I leaned against the island, clutching the sides of the mug as my fingers tapped against the sides. "Honestly, I don't know. My brother died a few days ago, and some people came back to my home for the funeral reception. I didn't know all of them."

"I'm so sorry about your brother. Maybe one of the people that attended was the purp. The question that remains is why would they target your home, or quite possibly you?"

I exhaled, "Thank you, Lieutenant, for your condolences. I have no idea who or why. I do know that my neighbors recently had an alarm system installed. I didn't ask any questions as to why they did it."

"Okay, I'll look into it when I get back to the station and I'll keep you posted on what I find. And you can call me Tony. Anthony Owens is my full name." He smiled.

I smiled back as I caught his gaze. He had a softness about him. He wasn't rough and tough like you'd expect him to be for a cop.

"I saw you at the cemetery the other day visiting with a loved one, I assume," I said as gently as I could. "I was visiting my brother's grave at the same time."

"Yes, that was the grave of my late wife, Nina. She was very sick and lost her battle with cancer. I try to go as often as I can. She died seven years ago," he said quietly as he bowed his head.

I gently winced. "I'm sorry for your loss, as well. I never thought I would be burying my brother. He was my best friend and I feel so lost without him. He was driving home, and the medics believe that he had a heart attack and that caused him to crash his car into the tree." I teared up as I said this. "I still can't believe that he's gone, and I'll never see him again."

He inhaled slowly, "I understand. Death is so final and for our loved ones to die in such a difficult way, just makes it harder on us." He said this as he placed his hand on my arm in an action to console me.

"Yes, that's so true," I said as a sob was stuck in my throat.

He cleared his throat and turned his head to the window. Curious, my eyes followed him as he readjusted. As if he had spent too long with me. "Listen, I'll check the perimeter again and look to see if I see any evidence that one of my guys missed, and then I'll be on my way," said Lieutenant Owens.

I nodded and watched him head towards the sink, "Thank you, Lieutenant. I appreciate that."

Slowly, he turned to face me as his lips hitched into a smile, "Please, Emma, call me Tony."

"Oh okay, thanks Tony," I smiled.

With that, he walked over to the sink and placed his mug into it. He reached out to shake my hand, our hands lingering for a little longer than I had expected, but it wasn't exactly unwanted. After we parted, I led him to the door.

"I'll be in touch, Emma. And please, do get that alarm system installed as soon as possible."

"I will. Thanks again, Tony." I shut the door behind him and double-locked it. As far as I was concerned, I will always double lock my doors from now on.

Dear Journal,

What is going on?! Someone tried to break into my house today. It scared the crap out of me! I don't worry about my possessions, they can be replaced, I worry more about Boomer.

HEAVEN FORBID, the guy got in and hurt Boomer! I'm sick to my stomach just thinking about it. Boomer is all I have left after Nate died. I could not survive another loss.

Lieutenant Owens responded to the call as well as his men that were in the vicinity. He was not what I expected for a cop. The direct opposite, actually. He was softer and caring, and he assured me he would catch the creep who tried to break in. Thank you, Lt. Owens!

~Emma

~Chapter 4~

The Salad

I glanced at the clock on the kitchen wall and realized that I only had an hour to get ready for my date. I wasn't even sure I should go now. But I felt it was too late to cancel.

I got ready quickly, and just as I was putting on my lipstick, I heard the doorbell ring, and Boomer went ballistic. He was barking like a mad dog. I guess he was reliving what happened earlier with the near break-in. I ran down the stairs and stopped just short of the front door. Grasping the doorknob, I went to pull it open when I had forgotten that I had double-locked it. I quickly threw the bolt back and grabbed Boomer's collar as I opened the door.

"Oh, hey there, fella," said Adam as he looked down at Boomer. Adam was a handsome man who had beady eyes that I hadn't earlier noticed in the dimly lit *Pork & Rind*.

Boomer kept smelling him, up and down his jeans and in his crotch. I hate that dogs do that, it's so embarrassing. However, Adam was a trooper through the whole interrogation that Boomer put him through. But Boomer seemed uneasy after he checked Adam over.

Red flag?

"These are for you," Adam said as he handed me a bundle of fresh flowers. They were beautiful. However, I noticed that his eyes did not meet mine, but instead lowered to the v-neck shirt I wore. I had to find a way to relocate them.

I cleared my throat, causing him to blink and look up at me. "Thank you, Adam. Did you pick these from your garden?"

"I stole them from my mother's garden, actually," he laughed loudly as he snorted.

Oh goodness! That is such a turn off when a man makes a snorting sound. *Geez, I sure hope this isn't a prelude to what's going to happen if I make a joke and he laughs at it.* That's such an annoying sound.

"Oh, okay. So, thank your mom, as well, for growing such beautiful flowers," I smiled.

He flashed me a weak smile in return. "I will."

I put the flowers in a pretty crystal vase my mom had given me years ago. The flowers fit perfectly. Adam walked towards the door. I kissed Boomer on the head and walked out behind him, carefully making sure I double-locked it.

Taking a moment, I eyed him, noticing that he was strutting towards the banged-up sedan.

I followed Adam to his car, where he opened up the door for me and dusted off the seat with his hand. I entered and noticed that his car was impeccably clean. I mean *really clean,* like OCD clean. There wasn't a need to dust my seat off.

Besides, who does that? Weird.

"I hear that *Donato's* has great chicken parmesan. Is that something you'd like to try, Emma?" As he locked the seatbelt into place, he was staring intently at me.

"Sure," I said uneasily, "That's one of my favorite dishes. How about you, Adam?"

"No," his reply was dull, "I'll probably have a salad or something."

I thought a little humor would break things up. "Why is that? Watching your figure?" I chuckled.

Well, what happened next was really strange and scary. He looked at me with the most piercing look in his eyes, knuckles turning white as he tightly gripped the steering wheel. He then pulled the car over to a screeching halt.

He stared out towards the distance before slowly returning his gaze to me, taking a tone I did not like. "Emma, I don't appreciate comments like that! Especially, when we barely know each other. And it's our very first date."

Okay, what is happening here?

"*Whoa,* Adam, step down a notch. I meant nothing by it. We are going to one of the finest restaurants in town, you can have any of the wonderful meals they serve, and you want to order a salad? What's with that?"

The inflection in his voice took on more of a stern volume. "Emma, I can order whatever I like. Do you understand?"

Oh, I got it, alright.

"Yeah, Adam, I get it. You can leave me off here. I decided I'm not hungry anymore." I go to open the door and he presses the lock button on the driver's door and holds it in place. The click of the lock rings through my ears frightfully. I can't get the door open.

I begin to panic, and I raise my voice louder, "*Adam*, unlock the door *now*! I'm getting out and I'm going to walk home. Do *you* understand me?"

He seemed to notice my attempt to leave. Quickly, he reached out, grabbed hold of my wrist, and pinned it to the seat. The squeeze was uncomfortable. "No need to throw a fit. Calm down, Emma. I want to take you to the restaurant, and we are going to go on our date as planned," said Adam, as he put the car into drive. But before he could drive away, my eyes caught hold of an unmarked cop car pulling up in front of him, and blocking the way.

It didn't long at all for me to register that the vehicle belonged to Lieutenant Owens. I felt relief wash over me as he approaches the driver's side with his hand on his gun that's still in the holster and asks Adam to get out of the car.

He inquired calmly, "What's the problem, officer?"

"It's lieutenant," he replied sharply, "You are under arrest for attempted break-in of a home and for voyeurism. Get out of the car with both hands in the air."

He continued to carry on nonchalantly, "What? I didn't do anything." Now it was Adam's turn to panic as Lieutenant Owens took hold of his wrists in a tight grip. "I'm innocent! Get your damn hands off of me!"

But Lieutenant Owens wasn't having it. "Turn around and stop your whining."

In a split second, my savior had him on the ground and in cuffs. I jumped out of the car and stood there in shock. I was so confused and had no idea what just happened.

"Emma, are you okay?" Asked Lieutenant Owens.

"Umm, yes, just a bit shaken up. He wouldn't let me out of the car. But… how did you know?"

He started speaking into his radio, and he called for backup. Within a couple of minutes, another cop car showed up with its sirens blaring. They took him into the backseat of the car and Lieutenant Owens turned and walked over to me.

"Emma, I saw him last night walking around the perimeter of your home. He was looking into your windows and was touching himself. He saw you walk past your kitchen window and he pulled down his pants and started masturbating. When I yelled to him, he took off on foot. I continued to watch your house and I saw him come back and try the back door again. That's when Boomer started barking and he took off."

The bile was rising in my throat. "Oh my God," I said as I put my hand over my mouth. I turned my back to him as I vomited into the grass. The lieutenant quickly reached into his pocket, pulled out a small package of tissues, and handed them to me. I wiped my sweaty brow off on my sleeve, feeling the dryness overwhelm my mouth. I couldn't believe what I had just heard.

"Come, Emma, I'll drive you home."

I got into his unmarked police car and sat there hunched over with my head in my hands. My makeup was running down my face, along with my tears staining the new silk blouse I had purchased for my date with this psycho. My ears were ringing, and I had a hard time hearing what he was saying.

"Emma? Are you alright?" His voice came in all distorted.

"I… no…" I muttered as I felt myself slipping into a black abyss of unconsciousness.

The next thing I remember is waking up in a hospital bed, not knowing why I was there. As the room came into focus, everything was in a blur, including the figure sitting upon the chair beside my bed. Initially, I took him to be the psycho. That was before he came closer, and my eyes adjusted to who it really was.

"Hi, Lieutenant," I said groggily as I opened one eye at a time in an attempt to focus on his face.

His blue eyes softened as his lips curled into a slight smile, "Hi, yourself. And what did I tell you to call me?"

"Tony," I tried to smile back. I repeatedly blink while I tried to center in on his face. I was still so confused as to why I was here. I had a massive headache, too.

"What do you remember, Emma?"

"I remember you were telling me that Adam was the one who tried to break into my home and that he had been watching me."

He nodded. "Okay, good. What can you tell me about the date?"

I attempted to recall the details, which were slightly fuzzy, and I began explaining slowly, "Well, he picked me up and gave me flowers. Boomer was sniffing him all over and seemed a bit uneasy. He kept stepping between us. Then, he opened the car door for me and dusted off the seat with his hand. I thought that was so weird because the car was impeccably clean."

With that, he gently chuckled. "Yes, I agree. What can you tell me about what happened leading up to the point when I pulled in front of his car?"

"We were talking about what we were going to eat for dinner, while we were driving to the restaurant, and he said a salad. So, I made a joke about it, and that's when he slammed his foot on the brakes and the car came to a screeching halt. I told him I wasn't hungry anymore, and I tried to get out of the car. He held his finger on the lock button so I couldn't open the door. And then that's when you pulled up in front of his car and blocked us in."

"Is there anything else you can tell me? How did you find this creep?"

"We met at a bar called the *Pork & Rind*. We texted but never spoke on the phone, which in hindsight should have been a red flag, I guess." Actually, now that memory serves me, he slid his number to me on a napkin amid the noisy chatter in the bar. We didn't talk much. I took a chance and this is what I got.

Though he didn't seem to judge me, he nodded once to acknowledge. "Yes, okay then, thank you. No need to worry about him now. He has been processed into the system, and if you will agree to press charges, we will make sure he stays in jail."

He didn't have to ask me twice.

"Yes, I agree to press charges. I don't know what I would have done if you didn't come along when you did, Tony," I sobbed uncontrollably.

As he took me in his arms to console me, I heard him whisper in my ear, that I would never have to worry again, and he would always keep me safe. With that thought in mind, I fell back to sleep.

I woke up several hours later feeling like I had to pee really badly. I pressed the button for the nurse to come and help me get up. I had a bunch of wires attached to me and an intravenous needle in my arm.

"Hello, Emma, I'm Maggie, your evening nurse. How can I help you?"

Again, I was groggy, antsy, and uncomfortable with a full bladder. "I need to get up and pee, but I see I'm attached to some things."

Maggie smiled warmly and replied, "That's fine, I can help you."

She untangled the tubes and disconnected the wires from the heart monitor that she said I no longer needed, and she helped me to my feet. At first, I felt a little dizzy. She explained that was normal and that she was here to help so I wouldn't fall.

Maggie walked me to the bathroom, which was right across the room from my bed, and she told me she'd be right outside the door if I needed her.

I felt better as I sat down to pee. I got up slowly when I was done, so I wouldn't feel dizzy again. I was fine. Maggie explained that I was severely dehydrated and that could be why I passed out. She also told me that I'd be free to go home tomorrow as long as I felt better, and all my bloodwork came back good.

However, something was missing.

"Umm, Maggie, did you see the gentleman that brought me in? Do you know where he might be?" I asked.

"Oh, your husband? Yes, he just stepped out for a cup of coffee. He said to tell you he will be right back."

My husband? Okay, my husband.

I laughed when she said it, and I figured he told her that so he could stay with me.

But why? Why would he want to stay with me? Was this part of his job? Or did he have another motive?

Just then, he walked in. *My husband in all his glory.*

"Hey, you," he said, holding a paper cup of coffee in hand.

"Oh look, it's my lovely husband," I smiled as I said it.

He wore a sheepish grin. "I can explain."

I was starting to feel better. "No need to, I get it," I commented as I began to adjust in the bed. "She probably wouldn't have let you stay if you weren't my husband or my family."

"Yes, exactly what I was thinking. So, how are you feeling?"

"I'm okay. I have a slight headache now, but other than that, I'm good." I looked into his beautiful eyes and felt he was so much more caring than I earlier took him for.

"I'm glad to hear that. I was thinking, when they spring you tomorrow, I can drive you home and check in on you in the next couple of days to make sure you don't need anything. How does that sound?"

Sounds like an offer I can't turn down.

"That sounds wonderful, Tony. And thank you so much for everything you have done for me so far. I don't know how things would have turned out if you hadn't been there to rescue me."

"You are so welcome. I'm just glad that everything turned out okay." And then, I saw Tony shift. The kind of nervous shift where a man puts his hand to the back of his head, eyes pinned to the floor, afraid to meet mine. "I was... umm... thinking. When you are feeling better, would you like to go out to a movie or dinner or something?"

Was he really...? He was. Okay, act cool.

"Yes, I'd love to. Thanks."

Just then, the nurse returned and explained that she had more bloodwork to conduct and added that I needed more rest in order to get better. Understanding, Tony had to return to the precinct to complete paperwork. He promised to call me later to see how I was feeling and would come back tomorrow morning to pick me up and take me home.

Leaving me with a gentle peck upon my forehead, he turned to walk out the door before turning his head over his shoulder to give me one last glance. It was a sweet and surprising gesture. It enabled me to see a softer side to him—a softer, gentler side, and I liked it. Very much so.

Journal!

Red flag, red flag, RED FLAG!

Why didn't I see this coming? What a psycho Adam was! I am so happy that Lieutenant Owens came to my rescue and arrested him. I don't know what I would have done, had he not pulled up when he did. I am eternally grateful to him.

He kissed me on my head before he left me in the hospital, vowing to come back to drive me home and to check on me the next couple of days.

It was actually kind of...nice.

How lucky I feel to have this man in my life. See Journal, good things do happen to good people, it just takes a little while.

~Emma

Till Death Do Us Part

~Chapter 5~

The Jerk

As promised, Tony called or came by almost every day to check on me for a week. He was kinder and gentler than he was when I was in the hospital. I automatically assumed that with being a lieutenant, he had to be coldhearted and unfeeling to fulfill his line of work.

One day while texting, I decided to tell him what I thought. He explained that he had to disassociate himself from his job, or else it would eat him alive. Tony admitted that he had spent two years in therapy working on doing just that.

I couldn't imagine working in that field, so Tony was a special kind of person to repress his emotions the way he did. I, for one, was far too emotional. But I can imagine that he's seen some things in his time spent on the force.

We made a date for the following week. He asked me what I'd like to do. I decided that dinner was a good place to start; we could talk more and get to know each other that way. He agreed. Tony said it was up to me where I wanted to go to dinner.

So, I decided that we should go to a pizzeria. *Ha!* He laughed so hard that night when I called and told him. He said that being dehydrated must have caused some sort of brain matter loss in my head. Tony never imagined I'd choose a pizza place. I explained to him that I *love* pizza, so what better place is there to take me for dinner? Besides, we can dress casually and just be ourselves.

He agreed that it was a superb idea when he stopped laughing. He also called me a *cheap date.*

I needed to focus on my work and prepare for my new job as a nanny for Leah's baby. She texted me a couple of weeks ago and told me she had the baby and she'd like to meet me in person. She said she wanted me to come by for tea and to meet her baby tomorrow. I told her I'd be there by noon and I was looking forward to it. She had no idea just *how much.* This was *Nate's baby! I'm so excited and anxious to see if she looks like Nate.* He's looking down from heaven watching over her, I am sure.

I am a little nervous that Leah will recognize me. But when I look in the mirror, I see a totally different person. This is what weeks of a healthier lifestyle will do. I am twenty-three pounds lighter; my hair is reddish auburn now and a lot shorter. I went from having long wavy hair to a short-angled hairstyle. My hair is shorter in the back and longer on the sides. *I love my new cut.* It's quick to wash and easy to dry. My natural waves even became more like curls now.

I bought a new pair of Michael Kors glasses and probably paid way too much for them, but I felt I deserved them. I used to wear contacts all the time. But they irritated my eyes and would move around, making my vision blurry. So, I switched to glasses, and I'm glad I did.

I even started dressing differently. I am dressing up more. Even if I was dressing casually, I would make sure I looked good, *really good.* I feel that all these transformations make me more confident, as well.

I walk almost every day with Boomer to the cemetery to see Nate, that's a long haul for the both of us. But now it's easier because Boomer and I are in much better shape. I feel great. And Boomer even lost a couple of pounds and built up some muscle. His legs look more muscular. Oh, how I adore this pup! He's the best pup I've ever had.

I was sitting on my chair at the island in my kitchen doing work on my computer when suddenly Boomer jumped up from his perch on the couch and went running right past me to the backdoor. He was growling and barking. The hair on the back of my neck stood at attention. I had a serious case of déjà vu. Boomer was going crazy. I picked up my phone and called Tony.

"Hey Tony, listen I'm scared. Boomer is barking wildly at my backdoor," I said quickly into the phone. I didn't even give him a chance to say *hello*.

"I hear him. I'm about two minutes out from you. I'll be right there. Let him bark. Make sure the door is locked and the alarm is set. *Stay away* from the door!"

"Okay, please hurry!" I cried.

I heard the skidding of car tires on the new asphalt that was put down on our street a couple of days ago. I knew he was here. There was a loud scuffle outside my backdoor. I was frozen in place, and now Boomer was really going nuts. I couldn't imagine what was going on. I then heard another car pull up with sirens blaring. I knew that jerk Adam was in jail, so what the hell was going on now?!

After about a half-hour, I heard Tony's voice as he was knocking at the back door.

"It's okay, Emma, you can open the door. It's me, Tony."

I scrambled to unlock the door. "Oh my God!" I said as I jumped at him and clung to him out of sheer fear of what just happened.

His arms tightened around me to comfort and assure me. "Hey, listen, it's going to be okay, Emma. It was Adam, he made bail and came right back to your home. Most perps return to the place of the crime they committed shortly after they make bail. I'm sorry this happened. But I am glad I was really close and could come over right away."

I hardly recognized my voice as they reached levels of hysterics, "I'm assuming I'm not safe in my own home anymore!"

He sighed and rubbed my back gently. "No, that's not true. It's all over, he will be tried harder now and not be released again because he broke his bail." He separated and held me at arm's length to look me in the eye. "You don't have anything to worry about, Emma."

I looked up into his eyes as tears fell down staining my face. He reached down and held my chin with his hand as he kissed me on the lips, deeply and passionately. I wrapped my arms around him and held on tight. I never wanted this moment to end.

I feel so safe, and so protected.

When we stopped kissing, he looked at me in near disbelief before a chuckle fell from his lips. I'm guessing this wasn't a normal occurrence.

"Well, at least we got this over with. Now our first date will feel so much less awkward."

A burst of deep laughter came out before I could respond. I couldn't control myself.

"Yes, that's always the hardest part. Let's do it again," I brazenly said.

Without warning, he pulled me into his arms, our lips met in a searing kiss as I found myself melting into him. I loved every minute of it. I can't remember the last time a man made me feel so good, so desired, and so safe.

He too soon parted from the kiss, "Emma, as much as I'd love to stay right here right now kissing you, I have to go back to work. I need to process this jerk and make sure all the charges stick."

"I know, Tony, but you are going to have to peel me off of you. I don't want to ever let you go."

"I feel the same way," he said as he slowly and gently released himself from my hold.

I reached up and kissed him deeply once again as if this kiss had to last me a lifetime, and then I let him go. He looked into my eyes and kissed me back quickly, then turned around and left. At the door, he looked back over his shoulder and winked at me. Then he was gone, closing the door softly behind him. I looked up at the ceiling and thanked Nate for sending me Tony. I feel it was all Nate.

I went back to my work. Just as I started typing, my phone rang. I saw Leah's number come up on the screen, so I answered.

Leah asked if I could come over today to meet with her instead of tomorrow. She sounded a bit frazzled with the shrill cry of my niece in the background. I knew I needed to get there sooner rather than later. I replied to her to give me a half-hour and that I'd see her soon.

I was already dressed and showered, but I wanted to freshen up and walk Boomer before I left.

I was ready in less than ten minutes. I kissed Boomer on the nose, gave him a treat, and walked out the door. I carefully looked around before I got into my car, just to be safe. I set the alarm remotely from my phone and I drove off.

Dear Journal,

Today I looked at myself in the mirror and I LOVED what I saw looking back at me. It was the reflection of an attractive, thinner, new, and improved version of me. I knew now that Leah would never recognize me and that my plan of being Grace's nanny will go over without a hitch!

My first date with Tony had gone better than I could have ever anticipated. I had never felt so comfortable with someone. Pizza felt like a five-star restaurant. I felt Tony really let his hair down and loosened up from all the hours he must put in at the police station. He and I delved into so many different topics, and many of them weren't ones you would typically talk about on a first date.

Journal, get this—he's like me, a hopeless romantic. He LOVES Hallmark movies. Like, we're talking cuddling under thick quilts with steaming cups of tea, and a blanket of snow outside. Just him and his special lady. It slipped that he could picture me as that special lady.

However, tonight ended poorly with that psycho Adam coming back to my home and exposing himself right outside my house while he looked into my windows. Tony came to my rescue again and apprehended him. He assured me that now the charges would stick and that I would be safe in my home. I thanked him once again, he has been my knight in shining armor.

~Emma

Till Death Do Us Part

~Chapter 6~

The Nanny

Leah's home was only about twelve minutes from my house, so I actually arrived six minutes earlier than I planned. I'm trying to park the car in front of her house when I glance at the house and see Leah standing in the doorway holding the baby. She's patting the baby's bottom and I can clearly hear that the baby is screaming. I quickly put the car in park, forgetting about how nervous I am, and I just about sprint to her door.

"Hi, Leah, I'm Emma," I said as I extended my hand to shake hers, my eyes nervously glancing over the wailing baby.

"Hi, Emma," she said quickly before practically throwing the baby in my arms. "Here, can you take her and see what you can do with her? She has been screaming for an hour now and I can't take much more of it."

I couldn't believe it, I was holding Nate's baby for the first time!

I readjusted my niece in my arms. "Sure. Here, take my keys. What's her name?" I asked with bated breath as my heart raced.

"Her name is Grace Angelina. Grace, because I've always liked that name, and Angelina was my grandmother's name."

"That's a beautiful name," I said as I walked carefully into the house holding the baby in my arms, looking down at her, and seeing Nate's features all throughout her face.

"Okay, so listen Emma, I trust you will take great care of Grace, and I am happy to have you. I can see she is calmer in your arms already. Let me show you where her bottles, diapers, and other stuff is."

Leah was rushing around like the Energizer Bunny on steroids. I had no idea what was happening with her. She practically threw the baby in my arms at the door. Now, she is hurriedly walking me around the house, showing me all I need to know.

"Okay, so do you have any questions, Emma?"

"No, as I stated in my resume and our texts, I am very experienced with childcare."

Suceess! She clearly had no idea who I was. This was a good thing. I'm not so sure she would have let me care for her baby if she knew my identity. After all, I didn't hide how I felt about her. Now, I wasn't just Nate's sister. I was a whole new Emma Porter.

She seemed to take little notice, or little care, I couldn't determine which. "Great. I'm going to go out for a few hours. My cell number is on the fridge as a reminder, so is the hospital, pediatrician, and other emergency numbers. If you need me, just call," Leah said as she flew out the door.

I just stood there wide-eyed, staring down at Grace as she looked up at me and cooed. I couldn't believe she was here. That I was holding my niece, Nate's one and only child he will ever have, and he isn't here to see her. A tear escaped my eye and landed on Grace's tiny pink nose.

"Hey, beautiful baby girl, I'm Auntie Emma, your daddy's sister," I said looking down at her. I found her eyes searching mine and holding me in her gaze. Lord knew she already had me.

As I walked through the house carrying her, I decided to take her into her room and change her diaper, it felt kind of full. I looked around the nursery, and oddly enough, it wasn't painted a pretty pink color like I expected. There weren't any pictures or anything hanging on the walls, either. As far as furniture goes, there was the bare minimum: a portable crib, dresser, and changing table. No rocking chair to rock Grace in, nothing.

How odd, I thought to myself.

I placed Grace on the changing table and changed her while looking at her, I told her of all the features she had like her daddy, "Grace, you are such a pretty baby girl. You look just like your daddy did when he was younger. You have his beautiful green eyes, and his small, pointed nose. You are such a cutie pie," I said out loud as if she could understand what I'm saying.

She looked at me with the biggest smile on her face, as she was kicking her tiny pink feet back and forth. I picked her up and hugged her tightly.

Then, I looked up at the ceiling and said a little prayer to Nate, "Hey, baby bro, here is your baby girl, Grace Angelina. Don't you just love her? She is all you, Nate. And her name is beautiful, as well. May God bless her and you."

I took her into the kitchen and heard the front door slam and a familiar voice calling out to Leah.

"Umm, hello?" I yelled back.

Then came silence. I heard footsteps slowly creeping down the hallway. I clutched the baby tighter against me as I listened further to put the pieces together. Venturing slowly down the hall, I heard the voice again.

I turned around to see Tony standing there, his gaze hardened with his hand reaching down for the gun at his belt. His hand twitched to react. I'm sure he was just as shocked to see me as I was to see him.

His eyes seemed to refocus, melting back into the soft blues I had come to know, upon sight of me standing there with the baby in my arms. "Hi, Emma," he said with relief as he walked towards me and kissed me gently on the lips.

I exhaled slowly as his hand moved away from the gun. "Hi, Tony, what are you doing here?"

He appeared perplexed. "I live here Emma; this is my house. What are *you* doing here?" He laughed as he asked.

"This is the childcare job I told you about on our date. Leah is the one who hired me."

"Oh wow, well I have a lot of explaining to do. But first, let's put baby Grace down for her nap. Your arms will be sore after holding her a while, she's a little chunky one," he said affectionately, as he lifted her from my arms and went to place her in her crib.

While Tony set the baby down for her nap, I ventured through the kitchen in search of any tea Leah may have had. I called out to Tony and asked him where I could find a box. After his instruction, I had a kettle boiling with two mugs ready.

"Well, hello again, beautiful lady," he said with my back turned to him. He must have been admiring me meandering about his kitchen.

I turned in my step to face him. "Hey, handsome," I said as I reached up and placed my arms around his neck while I kissed him with more passion than ever.

"Wow! What did I do to deserve such an incredible kiss?"

"Ah, nothing, I'm just glad to see you, and to meet Grace."

"Yes, I'm sure. Well, have a seat, Emma, and let me explain." He waited until I sat upon the stool by the counter. "I'm Leah's stepdad. I was married to her mom, and this was our home. When Leah had gotten pregnant, I suggested she move in here with me so I can help her care for the baby. Leah doesn't deal well with stress and let's face it, having a newborn can be very stressful when you're raising her alone. I felt I could be here to help with raising Grace, and to help Leah if she needed me to."

"That is very gracious of you. And yes, I detected that Leah isn't dealing well at all. I was barely out of my car when I noticed she was at the front door waiting for me."

He appeared concerned. "What did she say to you?"

"Not much, she just handed Grace to me as soon as I reached the door. Then she rushed me through the house, showing me where the baby's bottles are and other stuff."

"Wow, yes, it's been stressful for her. I think Grace has gas pains or something, too. So, I have been coming home early and doing paperwork at home so I can be here to help out. Where is Leah now?"

I bit my bottom lip. "I have no idea. She said she'd be back in a few hours. Tony, do you know who the father of Leah's baby is?" I asked cautiously.

"Actually, I don't. Leah said she didn't want to talk about it. Do *you* know?"

I nodded, fingers tapping against the sides of the mug. "Yes, Grace is my brother Nate's baby. I told you about Nate, he passed away…"

Tony flinched. "Oh, that's right, Emma, you told me about Nate. Again, I'm sorry. I had no idea Grace was his. This must be so difficult for you."

"It is… but I feel blessed to be able to be in her life even if Nate can't be. I know he's looking down from above and will always take care of her."

"Yes, I'm sure he is," he said solemnly, "God rest his soul."

Well, this was awkward…

But I had to tell him. "Listen, Tony, please do me a favor…"

"Anything…" he replied softly, "what is it, Emma?"

"Please, don't tell Leah who I am. And don't let her know that we know each other, or that we are going to be dating."

This was going to sound bad.

"Can I ask why?"

"I wasn't a big fan of hers and I'm afraid that if she knows who I am, she won't allow me to be Grace's nanny." This was painful to say. "We had words once, it was a long time ago. I look completely different then I did when she saw me a few months back at Nate's funeral—I was heavier, I didn't have glasses, my hair was a different color, and much longer. She didn't even recognize me today."

Though Tony appeared nothing but compassionate. "I totally understand. And for now, I'll keep it to myself. But eventually, we are going to have to tell her. Okay?"

As much as I hated the idea of it, he was right. "Yes, I get that, and I feel the same way." Saved by the whimpering of a baby. "Oh! I think Grace is up. I'll go get her and bring her back to see her grandpa."

Tony cringed playfully. "Now I really feel old," he said as he winked at me and then smiled.

As I handed Grace over to Tony, he smiled the biggest, brightest smile I'd ever seen. It was clear to me who the apple of his eye was. He coddled her and kissed her forehead several times. He was totally smitten by her, as was I.

Several hours had passed and finally, at 11 p.m., Leah came home and waltzed into the living room where we were talking. Grace had just fallen asleep in her baby swing, and Tony and I were whispering to each other for fear of waking up the little princess.

"Hey, Dad. Hi, Emma," Leah hiccupped. "Oh, I see you two have already met." There was a slur to her voice.

"Hello, Leah, where were you?" Asked Tony.

"Oh, just out at the *Shake-N-Stir* lounge with some friends," she answered loudly as she hiccupped again.

"Okay, let me put Grace in her crib and we'll talk when I get back," said Tony as he masterfully picked up Grace without waking her up, and carried her to her crib.

When Tony returned, all of the lightness had dissipated and was replaced with a darkened concern. His hands were at his hips as he addressed his stepdaughter. "Now Leah, what's going on? I can see you're drunk again, and you've stayed away for hours. I've repeatedly told you—you have a child at home now, and need to be responsible for your child. Not be out all day or night getting drunk!" Tony said sternly.

At this point, I felt like a third wheel. I tried to get up and excuse myself, but Tony raised his hand and motioned for me to sit back down, so I did.

"Oh, Dad, *stop*. I'm a grown woman and can do what I want, when I want. Besides, you said if I hired a nanny to take care of the baby, then that would free up my time. And I did. *So*," she said as she slurred her words.

Tony rolled his eyes and sighed heavily. "Yes, Leah, I did say that, but it was to free up your time so you can work or get your nails done. Not so you can drink and come home drunk! There's a huge difference here."

Leah appeared unfazed by his scolding, which to me was disrespectful. "Yeah, okay. Well, I'm going to bed. I'll see you tomorrow, Emma. Sorry about my grumpy dad, he's not always like this," Leah laughed.

I watched as she walked away and could no longer hear us.

It was Tony who spoke first, "I'm sorry, Emma, that you had to hear all that. Leah can be a wildcard, sometimes. She does what she wants and acts as though there are no repercussions. I didn't want you to leave so soon. Now that she's asleep, and so is Grace, would you like to sit outside for a few?"

"Yes, I'd love to. Lead the way," I said jokingly to lighten the mood.

"Yes, of course. Let me just get the baby monitor."

We left the house, the baby monitor gripped tight in Tony's hand. We walked down the length of the walkway, towards his car which was parked out in the street. He seemed distant, I assumed distracted from Leah's earlier display. I wasn't terribly surprised, as Leah had a tendency to ruin things every time.

Tony took me by surprise. Without warning, he turned to me and cupped my cheek in his palm, urging me towards him where my body instinctively leaned in. His lips eagerly met mine, flooding me with all of the feelings I had begun to feel for Tony. Was it so wrong to think that I wanted him to take me here and now? It had been a while since a man held me this way, made me feel wanted.

I was completely turned on by him. I reciprocated by tugging him to me, moaning into his mouth as the wetness began to saturate my panties, my thighs clenched together with every lasting moment of this kiss.

And Tony must have been a mindreader. Possessively taking me into his hold, he took my hand and shifted it to the crotch of his jeans. I could feel the bulge throb and harden, straining his pants. My fingers traced the length, surprised at what I discovered--little Tony wasn't exactly little. And perhaps his psychic ability was more of a curse than a gift at this moment, as he forcibly pulled from me. His breath was husky and ragged as he held me at arm's length. I recognized this, it was taking everything in him to restrain himself.

He wanted me as much as I wanted him!

"You turn me on so much, Emma. We need to stop here before I grab you, pull off your panties, and have my way with you." He smiled a devilish but sexy grin as he said it.

Oh. Wow.

"Mmm... We'd better stop before I let you," I moaned, "I think we'd better go back. I don't believe either of us can walk straight right now."

He kissed me hard one last time and then slowly shifted away from me.

"I never thought I could ever feel passion again after Nina died. But Emma, you have awakened in me things that have been dead for so long."

"They weren't dead, Tony, just lying dormant." I winked as I said it.

It only took a couple of minutes to readjust ourselves. He took my hand and held it as he walked me over to my car and unlocked my door. He opened the door and then spun me around and leaned in, so his body was pressing up against mine. Tony kissed me even harder than before, making me want him even more.

Round two? It was getting harder to not just give into this ravenous crave.

Huskily, Tony said, "Emma, I can't deny the attraction I feel for you. Forget dinner; let's go away, somewhere, anywhere."

I had to admit, I was impressed by the spontaneity. "Sure, I'd love that. Where and when do you want to go?" I said with a little too much excitement in my voice.

"I know you're watching Grace for the rest of the week, so how about next Friday after work, we leave for a long weekend and go off to Mystic, Connecticut? We can come back Monday night because of the holiday, and we are both off from work. That will give us three full nights together."

"Oh, Tony, that sounds perfect. I can't wait."

I reached up, kissed him deeply, hungrily, and wanted more than he could give me right now…

Dear Journal,

I did it. I pulled off what I thought was the unthinkable! Leah didn't recognize me, though I'm more concerned with what had her so distracted from caring for her own daughter. She didn't even seem interested in Grace! How could she not? She's a beautiful baby!

And as much as I want to write out paragraph after paragraph about Grace, I'm distracted, myself. I can't deny how attracted I am towards Tony. It's crazy. The way he kissed me makes me think that it's more than just a sexual chemistry...

To be continued...

~Emma

~Chapter 7~

The Wildcard

As soon as I pulled up into my driveway, my phone chimed, alerting me of a text message. I could not imagine who would be texting me so late. It started drizzling, and I wanted to get into the house and get Boomer so I could walk him before the rain started to come down. The weather forecast was calling for severe thunderstorms tonight.

Upon my doorstep, I took note of a package, which was odd, because I was not expecting anything to come in the mail. Kneeling down, I inspected the box and noticed that the return address was from Milan, Italy. I blinked with surprise and gingerly lifted the box, it was light! Shuffling the box in my hold, I knew I had to get it in as droplets began to hit my back.

I unlocked the door and Boomer came running almost immediately.

"Hey, boy, how are ya?" I reached down to kiss him on the nose, and he responded by planting sloppy, warm wet kisses on my chin. I placed the box down just beside the side table. He wagged his tail so fiercely that he knocked over my huge vase that was in the entryway. It contained the silk sunflowers that I bought last autumn at the county fair. Thankfully, the vase did not break, as the box broke its fall.

I grabbed his leash and put down my phone so I could quickly run him out. We made it back inside just before the first loud boom when the heavens opened up and the torrential rain began to cascade down. Boomer became startled by the sound and began barking ferociously. He was clearly unnerved. I took him upstairs and had him jump on my bed. Then I turned up the TV loud to drown out the sounds of the storm. After a half-hour or so, he seemed to calm down, finally relaxed, and went to sleep.

I put on my pajamas and it had hit me that the package from Caden was still downstairs. Hurriedly, I headed down the stairs to find the box waiting for me. Collecting it in my arms, I ascended the staircase and settled back down onto the bed, curling back up next to Boomer. That was when my phone chimed again. I had forgotten to check the text message I received earlier. I opened my phone to see who it was.

Although I was so tired from the day, I was so happy to see the text was from Tony. Multitasking, I opened the tape with one hand and the text message with another, nearly dropping the phone when I saw a drop-dead gorgeous pair of red Italian stilettos. Inside of the box was a card. I opened it up to read:

Sandy had a pair, and so should you. -Caden

Caden and I were big fans of the movie *Grease*. When he would come over, that was usually our go-to film. Where he first fell in love with the fashion of the 1950s, and where he made me swear I'd never tell that *Grease* was his favorite musical.

Granted, Sandy's heels were a backless pair. But I got the gist, and it was terribly thoughtful. I just nearly lost my breath and had to force my gaze back to the phone, which pinged again.

"Hey gorgeous, do you have plans for Saturday afternoon?"

76

I could not imagine why he was asking that, because we had just made plans to go away next weekend, and I did not expect to see him before then. I knew he had a lot on his plate with work, especially doing the paperwork to prosecute that loser whom he caught outside my house. I stole glimpses between the stilettos and my phone, tentatively pushing the box away so I could focus on Tony.

"Hi, Tony, yes! I'm free on Saturday. What's on your mind?"

"Well, I was thinking we could go to the county fair. It's the last weekend for the fair, and I thought it would be fun."

Okay, he wants to see me again before Mystic. That's a good sign.

"I would love to go. I was just thinking of the fair when Boomer knocked over the vase that contained the flowers I bought there last year. Boomer was so happy to see me, I guess. I was glad the vase didn't break."

"Oh wow, yes, he must have missed you while you were away from him. I know that feeling."

Oh my God.

"You are too sweet. Thank you." I typed as my heart raced with excitement.

"You're very welcome. So, I will pick you up at noon on Saturday. Is that good for you, Emma?"

"Yes, perfect, I will see you in a couple of days. Night, Tony."

"Sleep well, my Emma."

My Emma, really?

I must have fallen asleep right away because when I woke up, I still had my phone in my hand. Boomer was nuzzling my neck with his cold wet nose. *What a way to wake up.*

I laughed in spite of myself because I knew that when I sleep with Tony, he will not be waking me up quite that way.

Today, Leah wanted me to sit for Grace for a couple of hours while she went on a job interview. Leah had explained that she felt comfortable with me sitting for Grace and that she wanted to employ me five days a week after she got a job. She said she was hoping to work a 9-5 office job, and she asked if that would work for me. Of course, I said it would. For Nate's baby? I would do anything.

When I got to the house, Leah was again at the front door holding a screaming little Grace. I quickly got out of my car, walked up to her, and asked if I could help. With that, Leah just about threw Grace into my arms.

"Here," she grunted, "see what you can do with her. She has been crying for at least an hour now. I need to get ready for my interview."

I took Grace into my arms and held her close. I rubbed her back and she suddenly let out a loud burp. My guess is that she was extremely uncomfortable and full of gas. Once she let it out, she relaxed in my arms and closed her eyes.

Poor baby, I thought to myself, *Leah has no patience with her.*

I rocked her back and forth in my arms until she fell asleep. Then, I placed her in her baby seat, just as Leah came bouncing down the steps and announced she was off to the interview.

"Wish me luck," she said over her shoulder as she ran out the door.

"Luck," I mumbled curtly.

Leah was gone all day and part of the evening. I never expected to be here when Tony got home from work later that night. He was incredibly surprised to see me. He also seemed to have a look of concern on his face.

"Hello, my lovely Emma," Tony said, as he took me in his arms.

I melted, "Well, hello yourself. I could really get used to you coming home to me and hugging and kissing me this way.

"Good, because I really enjoy doing it," he said with a relaxed smile before kissing me again.

He is an amazing kisser and his strong arms always felt so comforting when he wrapped them around me. But I could see there was something on his mind, and it was distressing him.

"Tony is there something wrong? Is it the job?"

"No, it's Leah, clearly she's not home. It does not take all day to go through a job interview. A couple of hours maximum. Listen, Emma, you can go home now. I am here with Grace and I am sure I am going to get into it again with Leah. This sort of thing can get really ugly, fast."

"Tony, are you sure you don't want me to stay?"

"No, but thanks, Emma. Let me walk you to your car."

He walked me to my car and gave me a quick kiss on the lips. He told me he would see me tomorrow at noon when he picked me up for our outing to the county fair. I could not help but worry about him. He was feeling the stress of his job, and the stress of Leah. She was proving to be a wildcard for sure, and definitely not the motherly type.

Dear Journal,

Oh my God. I can't believe Caden sent me over a gorgeous pair of red stilettos. And all the way from Milan! He had even gone as far as to reference our favorite movie. ...He didn't forget. I feel so torn, because Caden had obviously put a lot of thought into his present, but then there's Tony asking me out and treating me like an absolute queen.

Journal, what do I do?

Then, there's Leah. I see she's making attempts to get her act together, but I think it's only because Tony is telling her to. She's still no more attached to Grace than last time. I'm getting worried because this could affect Grace later on. I can only hope that Nate is helping his daughter through this because I'm doing all I can on my end.

I only hope it's enough.

~Emma

Till Death Do Us Part

~Chapter 8~

The Courtship

Tony was right on time. I was just putting on my sneakers when I heard him knock at the door. I grabbed my purse and descended the stairs quickly.

I opened the door and there he stood with this sheepish grin on his face and his arm behind his back, "Good afternoon, Emma," he said as he reached out to kiss me.

Contently, I exhaled after we parted from the kiss, "Good afternoon, I'm so glad you're here."

"So am I, and these are for you," he said as he handed me a gorgeous fall colored flower bouquet tied together with an orange ribbon.

My eyes lit up upon receiving them as I clasped the large arrangement between my palms. "Tony, they are beautiful. Thank you."

Just as I said that he wrapped both of his arms around me and started kissing me, never missing a beat. He gently guided me to walk backwards towards my couch where he laid me down on my back, I dropped the bouquet onto the floor. Tony pressed himself against me and continued to push his lips against mine, probing inside them in search of my tongue. I felt his manhood arise to the occasion, as he pressed his body closer to mine. I trembled beneath him wanting him to go further. He grinded himself up and down on my thigh, making me shiver from pleasure.

Slowly, he raised his head to look into my eyes, arresting me with his gaze. "Emma, I am so attracted to you. I could take you here and now," he said in a groggy tone, "But I will not, not yet. It needs to be special."

I could not believe he stopped. I wanted him so much, I was so excited, and my mouth ran dry. He has such control over his body. Me on the other hand, not so much. I excused myself and ran upstairs to change my panties, for they were quite moist and uncomfortable to sit in.

When I came back down, he was sitting up on the couch petting Boomer on the head. Boomer seemed to be enjoying the attention as his tail thumped eagerly.

His eyes twinkled mischievously. "Are you okay?" He asked, smiling up at me.

At the bottom of the staircase, I stared at him dumbfounded. *The sneak knew exactly what he was doing.* "You have no idea what you do to me, Tony."

"Yeah, I think I do," he smirked. "You were not alone on that journey. Before I get crazy again, let us get going to the fair," he laughed.

"Sure thing. I'm ready and looking forward to it."

Tony stood up, adjusted the apparent bulge of his jeans, and was ready to roll. I kissed Boomer on the head and told him I would be back shortly.

Tony is a complete gentleman, as he always opens the door for me and holds out his hand to assist me in getting into his truck. It is a high step up and there are not any running boards on the sides.

I am super excited about going to the county fair with Tony today. There is so much to see and do. I am trying to decide what we should do first. Maybe we should eat, as my stomach is starting to gurgle.

Tony got a great parking spot, right near the entrance.

"Emma, I am starving. Would you like to get something to eat first?"

"Great idea! I was just thinking of that."

County fair food was always a treat. Between kiosks of games were a plethora of stands with goodies.

"I see they have hot dogs with the works and knishes too. Does that interest you?" He said as he grabbed my hand and led the way to the hotdog stand after I nodded in response.

"Yum," I said, "I haven't had a hotdog in forever."

"Great, what do you want on yours?"

"Why red onions, of course. Is there any other way to eat a dog?" I answered matter-of-factly.

"Nope! You are a woman after my own heart," he chuckled.

He ordered hotdogs, knishes, and sodas for us both. We sat at the picnic table and ate. The fair was not crowded just yet, as they had opened up shortly before we arrived.

The hotdogs were delish, and we devoured them quickly. From there, we placed our trash into the garbage can, and Tony took my hand again. He was like a little kid visiting the county fair for the first time. He wanted to do and see everything.

Our second stop was the basketball hoop game, where you had to toss the ball into the hoop and get it in two out of three times and then you would win a prize. You could win two small prizes and then trade them up for the grand prize.

"Emma, watch this," Tony said excitedly.

To my amazement, he got the ball in the hoop three times. Then he paid the guy to try it again. He did it again, and then a third time!

The kiosk attendant didn't appear too enthused, as though he had seen this done dozens of times before. Although, I caught his eyes lingering on me occasionally. Flushing, I had only hoped Tony didn't notice. Otherwise, there would be trouble.

"I'll take the big monkey with the heart in his hands," Tony told the kiosk attendant, then passed me the large stuffed animal. "Here ya go, Emma."

"Wow, *now* I'm impressed."

"Oh, I guess I neglected to tell you I won a scholarship for basketball in college," laughed Tony.

There was still so much I had to learn about him. "Umm, *yeah!* You must have been exceptionally good."

"I suppose I was," he mused. "Emma, excuse me a minute while I run to the men's room."

"Sure, Tony. I'll try my hand at the basketball game while you're in there," I said as I watched him turn and disappear behind the wall leading to the men's room. My smile was unyielding, his excitement infectious as I turned back to the counter of the kiosk.

"Hello, I'd like to try this game please," I said to the attendant.

"Why sure, pretty lady. Just give me a second and I will come over and give ya some pointers," he said.

Before I could protest, he jumped over the counter and was face to face with me. I could feel his breath on my lips.

He came up behind me and put his arms on my arms. His body pressed against mine in order to show me how to aim the ball. To ensure I would definitely get it into the hoop. His hands were at my waist, dragging down to my hips where they squeezed to keep me in place. I was totally uncomfortable with this and just as I was going to say something, I heard Tony start yelling.

"What the fuck do you think you are doing?" Said Tony as he grabbed the kid by the shirt.

"I, umm, was just helping this here pretty lady to shoot the hoops is all," said the kid.

"Well, now here's an idea, how about I take you by the seat of your droopy jeans and throw your ass *through* the damn hoop! Don't you *ever* touch any woman again the way you've touched my girlfriend. Do you hear me?" Tony yelled.

All the while, I stared wide-eyed that this was happening.

"Yeah, okay, okay! Get the hell away from me," the kid said to Tony and then he turned to me and said hurriedly, "Lady, keep that dog of yours on a leash!" He couldn't get away from us soon enough.

I turned to face Tony, who was about to respond, and I put my hand on his chest in a gesture to have him stop before this situation escalated any further. I told him we needed to move on. His face was bright red and his nostrils were flaring. He looked like a raging bull that just saw the red cape.

He took my hand and walked a distance away before speaking, "Emma, I am so sorry you saw that side to me. I was just so angry when I came up to you and saw him with his body pressed against yours and his hands on you."

"Tony, it's fine," I replied excitedly, "I could handle myself, no need to react that way."

"It's more than that. I was… a little jealous, I guess."

He said this with such disappointment in his voice. Disappointment with himself, I'd imagine. There was no questioning why. He was much older than me, not that attention needed to be drawn to that. There must have been some insecurity there between the folds of desire. I opened my mouth to respond before closing, shaking my head. He needed to know—know how I felt.

I took his hand into mine, squeezing it gently before raising it to press his hand to my lips. "I am yours and you are mine, Tony, have a little faith," I said softly, "There is no need to get jealous over some kid."

"Forgive me?" He asked sweetly as he kissed me tenderly on the lips. This was a difficult situation for him. He was not fond of public displays of affection either. Holding hands was fine with him but kissing out in the open was not something he liked to do.

It must have taken a lot out of him.

The rest of the day went well. We walked all over the fair and even jumped on some of the rides, too. It felt like we were young kids that were in love. He did steal some kisses in the haunted house where he felt no one would see us.

Private. Alone.

Tony won me another stuffed animal at the bottle ring toss game and he never left my side to use the men's room again. He seemed bothered by the fact that I saw the jealous side to him, but we did not speak of it anymore.

It was a perfect day, other than that little incident earlier. I felt so comfortable and at ease with him. It was as if we had known each other for a lifetime.

I glanced over at him while we were walking to the exit hand in hand, to see that he had a smile on his face that reached all the way up to his eyes. I wanted every day to be like this day.

Whether Tony realized it or not, he had won *me* over, completely.

Dear Journal,

Today, I saw a different side of Tony. It wasn't bad, per se. Just caught me off guard. I didn't take him to be the jealous type or to be insecure about our age difference. I wish he would know how that doesn't matter to me; I'm not looking at that.

But is he?

~Emma

~Chapter 9~

The Plans

Today seemed to go by so fast. I was really enjoying spending time with Grace; she is such a sweet baby. I wish that Nate was here now with her. I know he is in our hearts and one day when Grace is old enough, I am going to tell her all about him and show her pictures of us when he was little so she can see how much she looks like him.

I looked at the clock and saw I still had a half-hour before Tony came to pick me up. I was putting last minute things in my bag when my cell phone rang. I answered without looking at the caller ID and I put the phone on speaker.

"Hello?"

"Hey, Em, how's it going?"

"Umm, good… Who's this?" I asked, not recognizing the voice. Even though there was only one person who called me *Em*.

"I know we don't speak all the time, but I'm hurt you forgot what I sounded like," Caden laughed.

"Oh my God! Caden, I'm so sorry! How are you?"

"Better now since you know who I am. Listen, you seem rushed, did I catch you at a bad time?"

"Yes, I mean no… I'm going away for the weekend and I'm trying to pack, that's all. What have you been up to? Traveling again?"

"No, I am actually home right now. I wanted to ask you if you wanted to get together for lunch or tea tomorrow. But, since you are leaving, I guess I will catch up with you when you get back. How does that sound?" There was a pause before he added, "By the way, did you receive the package I had sent you?"

I heard the nervousness in his voice as my memory jogged back to sitting on my bed and marveling at the gorgeous red stilettos inside of the box. "Um, yes," I said cautiously, glancing back at my suitcase. "And they're beautiful! I'm sorry for not answering sooner, but I'm actually seeing someone right now."

He stumbled as he replied, "Oh! Hey, I understand, just wanted to send you a little piece of Italy. Just letting you know that you are always on my mind. Maybe we can catch up another time, no worries."

"That sounds great. Thanks, Caden. See ya soon. Buh-bye for now." I hung up the phone quickly before he could say anything else. I had to get ready, it was almost time to go. I still had to pack up Boomer's toys and food to bring to Adriana's house so she could watch him while I'm gone.

Adriana was a good friend and adored Boomer. I always felt bad when he jumped on her because she's a tiny bit of a woman who is 70-years-old now. Although she is spirited, young acting, and she doesn't look her age, sometimes I forget how old she really is. Boomer is a small horse and he can knock her right off her feet. I'm trying to get him to stop jumping up, but when he gets excited, that's what he does.

I heard Tony pull up. I grabbed my backpack with Boomer's stuff in it and threw it on my back. I took Boomer's leash and clipped it onto his collar, grabbed the handle on my suitcase, and out the door we went.

"Hey, beautiful," Tony said as he walked up to me and Boomer.

"Hey yourself, good looking," I smiled as I said it.

Tony kissed me gently on the lips and took my bag from me. He patted Boomer on the head and Boomer seemed to enjoy it.

He opened the back door of his truck for Boomer to jump in and he did so, almost as if it was on cue. I tossed the backpack in the back seat next to Boomer, hoping he wouldn't tear into it for his toys or food. We drove to Adriana's house talking amicably about what we were going to do once we reached Connecticut.

When we pulled up, Adriana was sitting comfortably on her front porch sipping her favored elderberry lemon balm tea. Boomer was going crazy in the truck because he was so excited and could see her from the car. I grabbed his leash, got him out, and walked him up to her house.

It was a big beautiful colonial home that had a wrap-around porch and large ceiling to floor windows. The house dated back to the 1800s, I think. She had it nicely decorated with fine antiques and other great items.

"Well, hello, Boomer," Adriana said as we approached her.

"Hi, honey, you look wonderful. As you can see, Boomer is just as happy as I am to see you," I said as I hugged her tightly.

I heard the car door shut as footsteps followed behind me. Tony introduced himself. "My name is Tony, it's so nice to meet you, ma'am."

"Oh, forgive me, Tony, I am so bad with introductions-this is my dear friend, Adriana."

"Nice to meet you, Tony," said Adriana as she reached out to hug him too, "Boomer and I have business to attend to, so you two kids get going."

"Thank you so much, sweetie. I'll call you when we get there and then again tonight to see how Boomer is doing. Everything you need is in the bag with a list of his feeding times. Thanks, so much, Adriana."

She hugged me, told us to drive safely, and said she will talk to me later. *I love that woman. She is a real gem.*

We got back into the car and set off on our new journey. I was quite excited by the whole process, going away with this man that I barely knew, but felt so much admiration and love for, I felt like the luckiest woman in the world. I thought that it would be this weekend that I was going to tell him—I was in love with him.

He and I spoke every day and every night about anything and everything we could think of, never having a lapse in our conversation. I find him to be the most interesting man I've ever met.

"Hey, penny for your thoughts," said Tony.

"Umm, nothing really... I'm just thinking about our little getaway. How about you?"

"Same. We will be there in less than an hour. I figured after we checked into the hotel do you want to go into town or to get something to eat first?"

"Well, since I'm always hungry, let's eat first. Then I was thinking we could walk around Mystic Seaport and go to the shops tomorrow. How does that sound?"

"Sounds like a great plan. I'm in," said Tony as he laughed.

As we chatted, his hand lingered over mine before interlacing our fingers together. Turning my head to him, he gently smiled and gave our hands a small squeeze. We arrived faster than we realized. It was so beautiful here. The hotel looked stunning from the outside. I couldn't wait to go in to see the inside. The hotel had this large cement sculpture of dolphins on the lawn in the front of the building that was amazing. The entrance was even grander than I had expected. It was beautiful, and I felt like I just stepped into another world.

This is definitely a hotel that I could never afford. I could only imagine how expensive the rooms must be.

I left Tony at the reception desk and I went exploring. I figured I shouldn't be there when he was checking in, because he was paying for the room and maybe he didn't want me there to see how much it would cost.

The first place I went to was the pool area and found a large indoor pool surrounded by these funky, yet comfy looking chairs, a coffee table, and some lounge chairs all colored in this bright pink color. There was a skylight above the pool that was huge and let in all the natural sun on this beautiful fall day. I loved this place already.

Then I moseyed on over to the lounge bar area, called *The Docks*. It had dual fireplaces and a flat-screen TV above it. The room was glowing with these muted teal lights that gave it a soft mystical glow.

As I was daydreaming and staring into the fireplace, Tony came up behind me and put his arms around my waist as he was kissing my neck, sending goosebumps up my back. I turned around to face him and kissed him hard on the lips. Nuzzling my nose in his neck and taking in the fresh scent of his Cool Water cologne, I whispered into his ear those three little words I was so afraid to say out loud.

Suddenly, without warning, Tony scooped me up off the floor and kissed me for what seemed like an hour. While he was still holding me, he whispered something into my ear, and I wasn't quite sure I heard him right.

"What did you just say?" I asked excitedly

I saw the sparkle in his eyes as he quickly replied, "You heard me."

"I know I did. Say it again," I probed.

"Marry me," Tony said even louder this time.

My heart was in my throat, pushing up the response that I couldn't say fast enough, "Yes! I *will* marry you!"

The moment was a blur. One big, exciting, important blur. It was almost as if Tony had this all arranged already. "Emma, how about tomorrow, right here in this hotel," asked Tony.

Oh my God, is this really happening? This only happens in Hallmark movies.

"Of course!"

His smile and gaze softened, almost with relief. As if there was a possibility I would say no. "Great, then it's set. Let's go ring shopping today, get you a pretty dress, and all the other stuff we need. Then if you'd like, we could have a celebratory dinner when we get back home with our friends and family. How does that sound? Oh, and we have to tell the hotel officiant of our plans."

"Oh my God, it all sounds wonderful! I'm so happy and excited. I love you, Tony."

"I love you, Emma."

We decided to go back to the front desk and speak to the receptionist, Betty, about getting in contact with the hotel officiant. She said not to worry, she would get all the necessary paperwork gathered up for us, and all we had to do was sign on the dotted line. Betty was extremely helpful and is almost as excited as I am. She said that they had a private room that they held weddings in and that she would book that room for us for tomorrow at noon.

I was so elated that I could barely contain myself. We decided that we should go to the Mystic shops and get our wedding bands first. While we were walking, Tony squeezed my hand, a little tighter now than he had in the car. Perhaps being engaged had this effect on him. "Hey, Emma?" He asked.

"Hm? What is it?" I turned to face him, taking in his expression.

"Did you happen to want an engagement ring or be proposed to on one knee? You know, traditionally? I know this is sudden, but I couldn't hold back any longer."

I knitted my brows together, "I don't need an engagement ring to be happy, nor do you have to get down on one knee. Having you is more than enough. Traditional isn't necessary, Tony. I love you, and knowing I'm going to be married to you tomorrow is all I need."

His eyes seemed to shine with relief, and I wondered if getting the bands would help make him feel better.

There was a fancy jewelry store not too far from Mystic, and Tony felt he could get a really pretty band for me there. I told him he needed to pick one out for me and surprise me. I didn't want to see it until we were to get married tomorrow. He told me then I'd have to do the same for him.

We both went our separate ways in the jewelry store. I walked over to a gentleman that looked to be about the same age as Tony. I asked for his help in picking out a wedding band for my fiancé.

It felt so strange to say that, and yet it felt so right at the same time.

He took out a tray of masculine-looking bands. There were bands that were black in color and made of titanium. I really didn't see anything I liked.

The store clerk took out the next tray of rings and there it was! Staring right back at me. I just felt it was the perfect ring for the perfect man. He took the ring out, polished it up, and handed it to me. The clerk also placed a magnifying glass with a light on it in front of me, and continued to explain the details of the ring. It contained five diamonds along the front side of the band that totaled one carat in weight. The band was made of 10-karat white gold, and had a medium thickness to it. I absolutely loved it. He tried on the ring and modeled it for me.

"Great choice," the clerk stated.

"Would you wear this band?" I asked him.

"Yes, I would. You see my husband bought us these matching bands that are similar to yours when we got married last year," he said.

"Perfect, thank you."

"Umm, miss? One more thing, what ring size is your fiancé?"

"Oh no," I laughed, "he's right over there. Please go ask him, I don't want to see the ring he has chosen for me."

"Sure, I shall return in a minute," he said as he walked away.

He was back in a flash, stating that Tony was a size ten ring. He said Tony wanted to make sure he has the correct size as well, so I needed to tell him so he could pass it on to him.

"I wear a size seven on my ring finger. Thank you for asking."

I gave the store clerk my credit card, and he said he would return in a moment. Then he asked if I wanted the ring gift wrapped. I explained that that wouldn't be necessary, and I thanked him.

Tony was done at almost the same time I was. He joined me as the clerk handed me my bag.

"Shall we go dress shopping now?" Tony asked.

"Yes, of course, I love to shop," I smiled a genuine ear-to-ear smile. My face started hurting from all the smiling I was doing today. I don't remember a day I was ever as happy as I am right this very minute. I don't want this feeling to ever end. I know with Tony, that every day we spend together will be a blissful one. Another thing I know for sure is that I have great instincts and they've never let me down. I can feel it in my bones for sure that this is the right choice. One I will live a *lifetime* to enjoy.

There is a lovely boutique that we decided to try out. Standing in front of the door, I wondered to myself if it was a good idea for Tony to be there while I looked for a dress. As if he knew what I was thinking, he draped his arm around me and whispered, "I honestly don't believe it's bad luck to see the bride in her dress before the wedding."

He called me a bride. Somehow, that already had me emotional.

Giving him an assured smile, we entered the quaint shop as my eyes immediately surveyed the number of dresses inside. The salesgirl approached us and introduced herself. Carrie asked when we were getting married, and was surprised when we unveiled that tomorrow was our date.

"Not impossible," she assured us as she looked me over. "I think I know just the one. I'll bring out that one, and a few others."

Tony released me to try on the selections. In the dressing room with Carrie, I tried on her suggestion and was head over heels in love with it. I knew Tony would be, too. It was a total classic! Reminded me of an antique off-white cocktail-length dress, that was full, frilly, and came to uneven points at the hem of the dress. This dress also had a lacy open back and three-quarter sleeves. I felt like a bride in it.

"He's going to love it," Carrie assured me as she squeezed my upper arms. "You're lucky. Not all grooms want to be here with their brides."

My smile was full and genuine. Stepping out of the dressing room, I came out to the platform display that had full-length mirrors surrounding it.

I once had an aversion to looking at myself in the mirror, but somehow--especially with catching Tony's awed expression in the reflection, I loved how happy I felt. I loved how *happy* looked on me.

Overcome with emotion, I felt the tears collect in the corners of my eyes, and roll down my cheeks. I couldn't stop. Tony rose from where he sat to collect me in his arms, turning me to him and embraced me tightly.

"Look at you, you are the most beautiful woman I have ever seen," he whispered to me, turning me back around to face the mirror. The two of us—together. "I can't wait until we get married tomorrow, and then I get to show you off as my wife."

"I love you, Tony, and I am so happy. I feel so lucky that you have chosen me to be your wife. Tomorrow will be a very special day that we will always remember. It's the beginning of the rest of our lives."

"Here, here," said the dress clerk, as she handed us both a glass of champagne.

"Cheers to our everlasting love, and to my beautiful wife-to-be, Emma, "said Tony as he stole a kiss from me.

This was the most amazing day, knowing tomorrow will only be better…

Dear Journal,

Should I feel bad that I let Caden down like that? He wanted to get together, and while I did want to see him, it's just that Tony and I are getting a little more serious now.

Serious enough to PROPOSE to me. Oh my God, Journal. It's an incredible feeling. To know how serious he is about me, how much he cares and loves me. We said those words to one another, and it was just as magical as I had imagined.

~Emma

Till Death Do Us Part

~Chapter 10~

The Desire

After our shopping spree, we returned to the hotel. The same receptionist was still there. She waved her hand vigorously to gain our attention, "Lieutenant Owens! Miss. Porter." I blushed at the change of suffix. It just made our engagement feel more real than it already did. "I wanted to let you know. The package you selected comes with a pre-wedding breakfast that'll be brought to your room at 8:00 a.m. Housekeeping should be by around 9:30 a.m. so that your room will be clean and presentable for...the night." She cleared her throat as she said it, causing a bubble of laughter to catch in my throat.

Betty continued, "The package also comes with Jose, our photographer. He's so sweet and does excellent work. We can't recommend him enough. I really think you'll love him. He'll take some pictures of you getting ready, Miss. Porter, pictures of the rings, the ceremony, you name it."

We thanked her and went up to our room. It was almost dinner time and I was exhausted from all the walking and shopping. Tony had suggested that we take a nap, then wash up, and get ready for dinner. I totally welcomed the idea.

I sat on the bed next to Tony, who was looking at the menu for the hotel restaurant on his phone, when he turned off his phone and stared up at me.

"I want to make love to you right this minute," Tony said suddenly, his comment catching me off guard, "but I feel we should wait until we get married tomorrow. However, there are *other* things we can do."

I was listening.

"Oh, is there now?" I asked coyly, "What may those things be?"

Without warning, Tony gently laid me on the bed, propping the pillows up behind my back, as he deeply sunk his tongue into my mouth, finding and dancing wildly with mine. His wandering hands roamed freely all over my body, which belonged to him—and only him. I reached down and felt his length growing and hardening against the zipper in his pants. I knew it wanted to come out.

I felt the wetness growing between my legs. I wanted to feel him inside of me… but he said he wanted to wait until we were married tomorrow. *Tease.* I didn't know at this point if I could wait much longer.

And perhaps we had a conversation that didn't require words. He seemed to know exactly what I was thinking. The slow tug of the zipper echoed into the strained silence. I barely noticed where his hand went, but my thighs pressed together tightly as his tallman slipped between the moist folds, eliciting a loud moan that I barely recognized as mine.

Tony chuckled. He *chuckled* at my expense. My thighs eased apart as his fingers beckoned to explore further, my breasts heaving as I struggled to gain control of my breaths—shallow and needy. My hips bucked against the palm of his hand, and my womanhood challenged him to give me his best shot.

The minutes drowned as ripples coursed through me, the pit of my stomach winding in a tight coil. I bit the fist my hand balled into, whimpering into it before Tony leaned down to cover his mouth with mine. The coil snapped as I came unraveled, my free hand gripping his wrist tightly as my moans were muffled with his mouth. I felt the rumble from his chest again, his lips parting from mine as I slowly came down from the high.

"Did you like that?" he whispered.

"Oh my God… that was *amazing*."

His hand soon departed from between my quivering legs. "Good, just wait till we are married tomorrow, and I will really show you how profound my love is for you."

He continued to kiss me and hold me in his arms until we both fell asleep.

I woke up to my cell phone ringing. It was Adriana. I realized I forgot to call her to let her know we had arrived. Because Tony was asleep, I decided to hush myself.

"Hello?" I answered with a whisper.

"Hi, honey, it's just me, Adriana. I wanted to make sure you arrived okay."

I winced. "I'm so sorry. I forgot to call you. We were just so busy since we arrived. We are doing great and it's so beautiful here. How are you and Boomer doing?" I asked.

"We are great, too. Okay, dear, I'll let you get back to Tony. Have a good time, I'll speak to you tomorrow."

"Thank you so much, Adriana. Love you."

"Love you too, dear. Goodbye now."

I hung up the phone and looked at Tony, who was still asleep. I thought it might be fun to *rouse* him from his slumber. It was even easier that he slept on his back. Carefully, I unzipped his pants and reached into them, cautiously withdrawing his penis.

Now, what should I do first?

I thought I would begin by taunting it, kissing along its length to get the blood going. Within seconds, it became as hard as a rock. I smirked, catching a quick glance to see what it would do to my love. With just the mildest clench of his eyes, I firmly started to stroke him from the base to the tip, then lowered my mouth over the head where Tony released an audible groan.

Wake up call.

My mouth replaced my handiwork (no pun intended), the wetness from my lips, and the strokes from my tongue had done their job. Tony reached downward to pinch my pebbled nipples through my shirt, twisting them gingerly as I moaned--in turn, vibrating against his shaft. It was a delicious chain reaction, leaving him to release my nipples and place both hands upon my shoulders. Slowly, he displaced me and rolled me onto my back.

He hovered over me as his steely gaze determined on his course of action. Leaning into me, he kissed me. His weight sank me further into the mattress as the sheets rumpled. My arms wound around him, legs wishing to begin wrapping around his waist as my body communicated exactly what he wanted. When he felt my leg graze against his hip, he leaned backward.

Not again.

Tony's chest glistened with a sheen of sweat against a body that appeared as though it hadn't aged. The image of his chiseled chest and abdominals left me hungry for something other than breakfast.

"That felt incredible…" he huffed, groaning as his member twitched admonishingly, "but I want to wait till tomorrow. I want to save it all up for you when I make love to you for the very first time."

"You have surprisingly marvelous control over your body."

"All for you, my love," he said as he kissed me again.

Dear Journal,

My fiance is a sexually charged 55-year-old man who just won't quit. He makes me feel sexy, wanted, and most importantly--loved. All of the ingredients to leave me excited and hungry for more.

He has so much control over himself. Maybe he can teach me because I can't hold out for much longer. I'm finding it harder to hold back.

All it takes is one kiss to ignite my flame. Which has been a problem since that first kiss. I've been daydreaming and fantasizing about moments like these, the little moments leading to the main event.

~Emma

~Chapter 11~

The Wedding

Tony decided that since it was getting late and we needed to be up super early tomorrow, that we should just get room service and have a quick dinner. I went to shower as he ordered the food.

As the water washed over my body, heated by the memories of the night before, I closed my eyes. They were the most pleasant memories I've had in a bit. Between Nate, Adam, and even Caden... *Caden.* I felt somewhat bad about how things left off between Caden and I.

My mind bumbled in a state of 'what-if'. However, the opening of the door caused me to jump as I was in mid-thought.

"Hey, Emma?" Tony called out.

Was he coming to join me?

"Dinner will be here in fifteen, beautiful," he informed me in a chipper tone before the door closed behind him. I felt the excitement of the moment fall into the pit of my stomach as I finished and toweled off, completing a quick change in a favorite t-shirt that I usually slept in.

Tomorrow, I will be Mrs. Emma Owens, I thought to myself as I stared into the elaborate bathroom mirror. *Mrs. Emma Owens.*

Turning the doorknob, I exited the bathroom to find Tony sitting in a chair at the desk across from the bed. Studying the itinerary for tomorrow, I'd imagine. However, the opening of the door caused him to pick his head up in my direction, soaking me in.

"Oh my God," Tony said as he sprang up from the chair.

Was the t-shirt no good? I didn't have any sexy lingerie on me. Was he disappointed?

"What? Listen, I'm so sorry I don't have anything sexy to wear for you," I hurriedly stammered, "I usually dress like this for bed."

Again with the chuckles. The husky laughter emptying from his chest, he collected me in his arms. "Oh, Emma! You *really* have no idea what you do to me."

Without warning, he swept me off my feet. Carrying me bridal style back to the bed where he began to address me with his lips, traveling down to my face, and following the pattern of my jawline to my neck. His hands proceeded with their exploration, to which I had little protest of. My body squirmed as while he held me with one, his hand traveled the smooth curve from my hip to my breast, cupping the mound in his palm as he gently squeezed. His other hand ventured between my legs to test the wetness that had pooled between them. The only barrier separating us was the fact he was still clothed.

I picked up from where we had left off the morning prior, wrapping my legs around him as I pulled him towards me, encouraging the hardness straining within the confines of his jeans to let instinct pave its pathway. I wanted to feel him. I craved it.

I became so excited that I wanted him inside of me. I knew he wasn't going to do it because he wanted us to be married first. But he was driving me wild. So, it was me who had to stop him now. I couldn't let him go on, because I would have lost control easily.

It was so apparent that he and I had very high sex drives and we were strongly sexually compatible.

"Tony, no," I groaned, "I know you want to wait until tomorrow, and I respect that. If you keep doing what you are doing, I'm going to lose control."

"Emma, you are so incredibly sexy, and you have no idea how much I desire you. I want to crawl up inside of you and never come out. That t-shirt with nothing under it is the sexiest thing you could have ever worn. You have me so turned on, feel me, I'm hard as a rock, again. Please don't ever do that again, or I will lose control and have my way with you."

I laughed hysterically at what he just said. This man must really love me, for he sees me as being sexy in a plain white t-shirt that says *Dog Lover* on the front of it. This really told me a lot about him, it meant to me that I didn't have to dress a certain way to turn him on. He was more excited by knowing I had nothing under the shirt. I knew in my heart that the best was yet to come. Tomorrow was going to be the most exceptional day of my life!

The food finally arrived, and we ate and then sat in bed to watch a movie on Netflix. We were both exhausted from the day and our stomachs were full of the heavy pasta we just ate. Knowing we had a full busy day ahead of us, we only watched about an hour of the movie before turning off the TV. Tony and I kissed goodnight and I cuddled up to him in his arms and he fell asleep almost immediately.

My alarm went off at 6:30 a.m. this morning, and I jumped up to start getting ready by doing my hair and makeup. I didn't wake Tony until 7:15 a.m. He really didn't need to do too much to get ready for today. The food came as scheduled at 8:00 a.m., and we enjoyed a delightful breakfast together. I drank a couple of mugs of tea, and he had his usual large mug of coffee. Then I went to finish getting dressed in my beautiful dress and shoes, I came out of the bathroom and Tony was already in his light blue suit that brought out the color in his eyes even more.

He was positively stunning.

"My goodness, you look incredibly beautiful on our wedding day," said Tony.

I gave him a turn, feeling myself glow. "I am so proud to be marrying such an amazing and handsome man like yourself, Mr. Owens."

"I'm the luckiest man alive," he said as he gently kissed me on the cheek.

Just then, there was a knock at the door. The photographer arrived fifteen minutes early, which was fine because we were both dressed and ready for him.

A youthful young man stood at the door with a bright white smile. His mouth stretched from ear-to-ear against his caramel skin tone. Between his palms rested a professional-looking black Nikon camera. "Hello, sir. I am Jose, your photographer."

"Very nice to meet you, Jose. And this is my soon to be wife, Emma."

The photographer shook our hands and congratulated us. His chocolate eyes scanned the room, assessing lighting and backdrops before instructing us to first stand in front of the large picture window with the curtains closed. He explained that the curtains would make a beautiful backdrop. Then, he wanted our rings so that he could place them in front of my bouquet on the table. Tony interjected that we had yet to see the rings, and we had no intention to see them until the ceremony. That didn't seem to be a problem for Jose.

The next hour we kept busy with taking photos in the room, then proceeding downstairs and into the lobby where Tony had proposed. All I heard was the snapping and clicking from his camera.

We took a short break before the ceremony, which gave enough time for Jose to run us through his plans. He joked that he was our shadow, and would be ours for the day. Tony and I expressed that we were going to dinner in a fancy restaurant down the road, which was fine by him. He would follow us there and take additional pictures. Tony had even offered to buy him dinner for his services that would run later into the evening.

Jose took so many pictures, but he wanted to give us options that he would e-mail over and offer packages of what we'd like, advising us further that it would be a three to four-month process. The last step was to choose albums and sizes that he would then assemble for us. I never realized before what a process this was. Tony thanked him and tipped him an extra hundred dollars. Jose was grateful, as he took this job to pay for his college expenses. He hugged us both tightly.

The officiant, Jayden, was a young African American man, who told us he performs weddings for the hotel part-time while attending medical school. He told us he comes from a long line of doctors in his family, his Mom is a pediatrician and his Dad is an oncologist. This young man already impressed us before he even started our wedding.

Jayden told us where to stand and what to do. He instructed the photographer where to stand as well. He made some suggestions to Jose as to where he should shoot from because he understood how important lighting and getting the right angles were.

As we took our positions, the receptionist and the photographer agreed to be our witnesses.

At exactly noon, the ceremony began.

"Friends and acquaintances, we are gathered here today to celebrate love and unity. The respect of vows and bringing together love—the greatest force that can and will transcend time. Today, we bring together Emma Porter and Lieutenant Anthony Owens in holy matrimony. The couple has vows they'd like to promise to one another. Lieutenant, would you like to go first?"

We both recited the vows we had chosen to pledge to each other.

Tony admired me, gazing into my eyes. "Emma, I never thought I would love again after Nina. And then you came into my life and proved me wrong. You've proved me wrong about many things. That I'm not too old to give love another chance, that there is still fight left within me. My heart beats for you, I promise to live for you, to honor and cherish you in the ways that you deserve to be. To dedicate my life, till death do us part, to giving you all that you will ever want and need. To this I vow, I love you, my Emma."

I had never heard more beautiful words. Nor have I ever seen Tony's eyes glimmer with tears, throat thickened with emotion. It was a rare event, one that was reserved for me—and possibly even Grace.

Had Nate really conspired this from above? I sucked in a slow chunk of air as I could have sworn I saw Nate standing behind Tony. A smile on his face as he nodded and urged me to speak.

But my voice was already lost as Jayden turned to me, "That's hard to follow up." Tony, Jayden, and even Jose laughed. "Tony, I was beginning to give up on love, and thinking that time was against me. And then you literally tackled my doubts to the ground. I think Nina and even Nate had a hand in our meeting. Love has no time, no reason. You've made me a believer that true love is possible. I didn't need months or even years to know...to know that you are my perfect man. I vow to kiss you every morning so that you may have a safe day, and a kiss for every night you returned to me. I give you my heart and my soul. I love you, Anthony Owens."

Even Jayden had tears in his eyes before continuing, "Do you, Emma Porter, take Lieutenant Anthony Owens to be your lawful wedded husband?"

"I do," I barely uttered.

"And do you, Lieutenant Anthony Owens, take Emma Porter to be your lawful wedded wife?"

"I most certainly do," declared Tony.

"With the power invested in me, I now pronounce you husband and wife. You may now kiss your bride."

With that, Tony tipped me backward, while holding me in his strong arms, and kissed me deeply in front of our witnesses. It was the most amazing moment of my life.

They all congratulated us and wished us well. We informed the photographer as to where we were going to dinner and gave him the directions to get there.

They all hugged us and we then exited the room. Outside, a small crowd had gathered. I'm assuming because they saw me enter the room in my wedding dress. They all congratulated us, and some people hugged us. I was so proud to walk out of that room with Tony on my arm. As I glanced over at him, he too had a huge smile on his face that warmed my heart.

"Come on, Mrs. Owens, we have some celebrating to do," Tony said as he pulled me closer to him.

"Why yes, I do believe we do, Mr. Owens. And by the way, I love the sound of that."

We jumped into his truck and drove a short way down the road to the restaurant. From the outside, it looked exclusive, and I could only imagine what the inside was like.

He came around to my side of the truck. Upon opening the door, he took my hand to help me out. *Walking in these glittery white heels was a killer.* After, he spun me around and gently pressed his body against mine, leaning me further against the cool paint of the truck that was ebbing my heated body. My eyes widened in surprise as I felt his length harden. It was truly amazing how he felt so sexually attracted to me. That alone left me supercharged and wanting more.

The parking attendant cleared his throat several times, as a hint for us to break it up. When I finally suggested to Tony that we head into the restaurant, I looked up to see a whole line of cars waiting patiently for the same parking attendant. We both laughed in spite of ourselves and thanked the attendant, then walked inside.

The place was even more spectacular on the inside then it was on the outside. Beautiful white roped lights surrounded the dining area. The wait staff were all dressed well in white tops and black dress pants. The hostess was dressed in a formal gown. I was very impressed with what I saw.

I was hoping the food was just as good.

We were seated by the large window that looked out over the water and the sun was just beginning to set. Jose arrived shortly after we did, and he suggested that we all gather outside quickly to take pictures by the water with the sun setting in the background.

He had us posing in all sorts of different ways, and all I kept thinking to myself is *wow, these are going to make beautiful photos.* We were done within a few minutes and then went back inside to order our food. Jose explained that he would continue to take random pictures and that we should just *act natural.*

The waitress came back to give us a bottle of champagne on the house and congratulated us on our wedding day. I thought that was really sweet. We placed our dinner order with her and then we toasted to our long life together.

I still felt as if someone should pinch me and wake me up from this wonderful fantasy. I never would have thought my life could be as wonderful as it was now.

The food was exceptional, as expected. We both ordered the filet mignon, with a side order of roasted potatoes, and a house salad.

What's funny is that we learned so much about each other in such a short period of time, but yet we never thought to ask each other what our favorite foods are. Or how we like our steak cooked. He likes his rare, I like mine very well done, almost burnt.

We do, however, have the rest of our lives together to figure out all the other stuff.

The manager of the restaurant came over personally to introduce himself to us and ask what kind of cake we liked. He gave us three choices. We both picked red velvet. Then he returned shortly afterward, with a mini three-tiered red velvet wedding cake with a flower to serve as a cake topper, he shook our hands and congratulated us.

"Wow, just wow! I can't believe that they did this for us," I said.

"Yes, it is wonderful isn't it, Emma?"

"Tony, this really has been such a magical day, one we will talk about for years to come."

"I agree. Now eat up and let's get back to our room, where we have more celebrating to do. I'll order an extra bottle of champagne. The bubbles seem to get you giddy," winked Tony.

I laughed out loud and hiccupped! I was so embarrassed. At this point, I wished I was a turtle and could hide my head in my shell.

Dear Journal,

May I introduce to you the new Mrs. Emma Owens. In 72 hours, I've gone from girlfriend to wife. And the feeling is incredible, indescribable.

I had been working on my vows in my head since Tony proposed, however, he blew me away with his. I had no idea he felt that way. Truly, I am the luckiest woman in the world. He makes me feel special, wanted, loved, and desired. More so than I've ever felt with a man. I know I've said this in past entries, but I am over the moon with excitement.

I feel like I'm living in a dream, a real-life fairy tale. I know, I know, I'm a writer who lives off of cliches, but—I have no other words.

~Emma

~Chapter 12~

The Honeymoon

We got back to the room rather quickly and Tony insisted on carrying me over the threshold before placing me on the bed. After kissing me for several minutes, he suggested I get out of my wedding dress and hang it up so it wouldn't get wrinkled. Beneath him, I felt sheltered and safe. The way a person should feel with their beloved. I didn't care about wrinkling my dress, there was always dry cleaning.

"I'm going to get undressed. Why don't you make yourself more comfortable, Mrs. Owens?"

I may have released a minor groan in protest, but as I sat up on my elbows, Tony had disappeared to disrobe.

I got undressed in the bathroom and placed my dress on a hanger. I untied my updo and let my curls fall and land on the top of my shoulders. I brushed my teeth and sprayed a bit of my favorite perfume, Burberry, behind each ear, and on my wrists. I touched up my make up and put bubblegum lip gloss on my lips. I knew he would kiss it off right away, but I figured he would enjoy the taste along the way. I took one last look in the mirror and liked what I saw. I saw the new Mrs. Owens in all her glory.

I turned out the light and shyly walked out naked to meet my new husband already in bed.

"Oh my, Emma. You are so beautiful. Let me look at you," said Tony.

Instinctively, I covered up, one arm crossed over my breasts. The other over my nether region. "Tony, stop, you're embarrassing me."

He frowned, then. One of the first times I had ever seen him truly frown at something I had said. "Emma don't ever be embarrassed in front of me about anything. I love you and you are a beautiful woman, not just any woman—you are my woman, my wife, my lover, my everything."

Tears welled up in my eyes as he said that. I can't remember any time in my life that a man had ever said anything so loving and kind to me. His words and his actions reinforced to me just how much he loves me.

He got up, walked over to me, and took me by the hand. He put soft, romantic music on his phone and asked me if I would like to dance with him. I felt kind of awkward, we were both standing there fully exposed. But he didn't seem to care. I needed to remember with him that there is no room for my shyness. He is a very open, relaxed, and confident man, and that's what I love about him most.

He took me in his arms and held me close, I could feel his erection as it prodded at my body. We danced and twirled all around the large room. At this point I felt like Cinderella, and what she must have felt when she danced at the ball. He made me feel like I was the most stunning woman in the world.

Tony led me over to the bed and had me sit on the side of it. He then reached into the nightstand drawer.

"Here, this is for you, my lovely bride."

"Tony, what's this?" I asked.

"Well, it's your wedding gift."

"Oh no, I didn't get you a gift," I gasped.

"Emma, I just want you to know how much you mean to me. I will spend the rest of my life loving you and spoiling you too. You might as well just get used to it," he laughed.

I opened up the box to find the most beautiful white gold heart-shaped locket with sparkling diamonds all around it. Inside the locket was the inscription:

My heart belongs to you. ~T.

With that, I lost it and started crying all over again. He placed the necklace around my neck and hugged me closely. He told me he just wants to make me the happiest woman in the world and to keep me happy forever. And he has done that from day one!

My husband wiped away my tears and kissed all the places on my face where they landed. He then lifted my legs onto the bed and placed them under the blanket. My husband then handed me a glass of champagne and then got into the bed on his side. We toasted to a happy long marriage and finished our glasses.

Tony got on top of me and pushed back the blanket so he could see all of my body in the dimly lit room. He started kissing the weak spot on my neck, which I felt must have a direct line connected to my personals. When he does this, I'm instantly aroused.

He worked his way down my body, kissing every inch of it—claiming it officially as his own. Between his teeth, he collected the pebbled nipple, licking and sucking on my breasts until I moaned. Reaching down between my legs, his tallman flirted with my nether regions and I barely recognized my own moans.

Rolling me over onto my stomach, he arches my bottom up in the air; all the while, he didn't miss a beat with his kisses. He continued to kiss up my back and buttocks. I felt like I was in some sort of trance.

I was enjoying everything he was doing to me when I thought I heard the sound of clanking metal. Tony gently stretched my arms out in front of me, moving them more widely apart from each other. I had my eyes closed and felt a coldness on both of my wrists. I briefly opened my eyes to see that he was handcuffing me to the bed.

Oh my God! This was a huge turn on.

He was kissing my sweet spot from behind, sticking his warm tongue in places that were never touched before. I squirmed enthusiastically, indulging myself in pleasures that I never thought I could experience with another. His hands took purchase upon my hips as he steadied me, guiding himself inside to which I hitched my breath. The moment we both had been anticipating had finally come. My walls clenched around him, enticing a groan from deep within the back of his throat. Slowly, he withdrew, then slid back into me, creating a rhythm that was all our own.

However, it didn't take long before he picked up his pace. I gasped, burying my face into the pillow as he began to push deeper within me, angling my hips in such a way that sent a shiver through me. Immersed in indescribable pleasure as it surged throughout the entirety of my frame. My moans heightened to cries.

Cries evolved into screams as Tony's hands squeezed my hips, reaching down to slap at my rear as he leaned in and

126

kissed the space between my shoulder blades, propping his hand upon the wall just beside my head to steady us both.

For our first time, this was a hell of one.

I leaned my head back as Tony stretched to kiss my lips, pulling me down further with his strong hands against him. One hand abandoned its post to reach around to the front of me and between my legs. It didn't take long until I came in rolling orgasms. And it seemed when I had peaked, Tony did, as well.

Another thing we can say we did, together.

He reached up above me and unlocked the cuffs with trembling hands. I rolled over to look at him and saw he was just as spent as I was.

"That was incredibly…amazing," I said breathlessly.

"Umm…so you liked it, huh? I took a chance, hoping you would. I'm so glad I pleased you, Emma."

I looked at him with disbelief. "Not just once, Tony…"

All of a sudden, it occurred to me—that we didn't use protection! I could have just gotten pregnant. I'm way too old and this ship has sailed. I just turned 35 a couple of months ago, and Tony was 55!

"Oh my God," I said out loud as I bolted upright in bed.

"What's wrong, honey?"

I nervously replied, "Umm, Tony, I just realized that we didn't use protection, and you just came inside of me."

He didn't seem bothered by this. Rolling onto his side, he supported himself up upon his elbow. "So, what's the problem, Emma? We're married, you work at home mostly, and at my home with Grace, too. *So what* if you got pregnant? We'd have a child of our own."

I sat up, clutching the blankets around me as I brought my knees to my chest. How could I have been so careless? "We never spoke about kids. Would you want a child, at our ages?"

But there was Tony, ever the rational one.

"Emma, you make us sound so old. Women are having kids *way* past the age of 40 now. Besides, it would be nice to have a child of our own and we could raise him or her along with Grace. They would be built-in playmates."

"Wow, you make it sound so easy," I half-laughed. "I never really gave much thought to having kids because I never found anyone to love, the way I love you."

"I love you, too." It was then he reached for me, sitting up to collect me in his arms. "Don't worry and let things fall where they may. We don't know if you got pregnant tonight, you might not have. Relax, Emma, and let's sleep."

I cuddled up to him and the next thing I knew it was morning.

I awoke lying next to the man I just met only a few months ago, fell in love with, and married. I may even be having his child, who knows. One thing I do know for certain is that I adore him, and he clearly adores me. I feel we are destined to have a wonderful life together.

Dear Journal,

Once upon a time ago, I didn't like what I saw in the mirror. I was afraid to show myself to others and felt ashamed. Loving myself was a key element to overcoming it, and that came through working on myself. That opened me up to accepting others in.

Tony has proven to me that I needn't be ashamed of myself. The right one will never make you feel less than, and I feel Tony raises me up.

Remember how I mentioned he treated me like a queen? He gifted me with a cherished wedding present of a beautiful locket with an inscription I'll take to heart. Because we gave parts of one another to each other, and now I'm carrying a piece of him with me.

~Emma

Till Death Do Us Part

~Chapter 13~

The Homecoming

We packed up and went down to have breakfast before we checked out. I called Adriana to see how she and Boomer were doing. She said they were both doing well. Tony and I decided that we would go to the Mystic shops again after breakfast, and then we would head home. I wanted to pick up a little gift for Adriana and Boomer if I could, to give them when we arrived back home.

Tony and I literally shopped our butts off. I was exhausted and needed a pick-me-up. So, we looked for a place to stop. We found a little cafe and decided to sit down and grab a cup of tea for me and coffee for him. They also had awesome homemade crumb cake and we grabbed a slice of that as well. After spending about twenty minutes there, we decided we better get going so we don't hit too much traffic on the way home. I was anxious to go see Boomer and of course to see Adriana.

I couldn't help but think about my life now and how it's changed drastically in the past 72 hours. I had no idea how I was going to explain to anyone that I went away for a weekend with my boyfriend of a couple of months and came back married. I wasn't so sure that I was going to tell anybody right away, either. This is something that Tony and I hadn't even discussed yet. There was so much more to talk about: where we were going to live, was his stepdaughter and Grace going to come and live with us? Were we going to live in my place or his? Lots of decisions to be made when we got back home.

"Emma, I was thinking, how about if we sold both of our homes and bought a new home together? What do you think?"

What is he, psychic?

Alright, out with the old and in with the new.

"I think that's a wonderful idea. I was literally just thinking about the fact that we didn't even discuss this yet. We could live in my town because it's closer to your job."

He seemed to mull this over, turning his head from side to side pensively. "Yes, I suppose so. If you don't mind, it would make things easier."

"Of course," I said as I reached over and kissed him, "anything for my husband."

"Great, then it's settled, when we get back home, I'll call a realtor friend of mine and we can list with her."

The rest of the way home we chatted about our plans. He is such a positive person like me, and I feel we will be a great team together, there is nothing we can't handle.

"Hey, Em! How are things?"

Caden had texted me and I really didn't want to answer right now. I was so caught up in the beginning stages of our marriage. I really didn't even know if Tony was going to be jealous of my relationship with Caden, or if he had a problem with me having male friends no matter who they were.

Eventually, I would tell him about Caden and what he means to me.

"Here we are, back again," said Tony as he pulled into Adriana's driveway.

Boomer was on the deck, barking and wagging his tail wildly when he saw us pull in. He's one smart dog and he knew who it was in the truck. I could not get out fast enough to go hug him. I tripped on the way up the stairs and I guess Boomer must have thought I was hurt because he busted right through the gate that held him back and he came to my aid before I even got up.

"Hey boy! How are you?" I said as I pet his head and hugged him tightly, "I have missed you so much!"

"Emma! Are you alright?" Tony asked as he helped me up.

"Yes, I am such a klutz," I laughed.

Adriana got off the porch to greet me and Tony went to see what he could do about the broken gate.

"Hi, Emma, my goodness, you need to be more careful. You scared me half to death," said Adriana, "How was your trip?"

While to Adriana, my blush could have been from embarrassment, there was another reason. Tony and I exchanged a knowing glance as I smirked. "It was fabulous. In fact, I have some wonderful news- Tony and I got married yesterday!" I waited to see her reaction. "I know what you're probably thinking, that I've only known him a couple of months or so, how could I have possibly been crazy enough to marry him. Honestly, I feel, as an adult of 35 years, I know what's right from me at this point in time, and I know who's right for me."

Adriana, at first, didn't react. She stared, her eyes drifting from me as I spoke, over to Tony, and then lingered back over to me. Her lips spread widely.

"Oh, Emma, I am so happy for you! That is wonderful news! You really don't have to explain anything to me. I know what a smart woman you are and that you went into this with your heart and your head. Congratulations honey," Adriana said as she hugged me tightly.

"Thank you so much, Adriana, I knew you would understand and not judge me. So, tell me how was Boomer for the past couple of days that we were gone? Was he a good boy? We bought both of you a gift from Mystic, Connecticut. Let me tell you, it's really pretty there and the shops are fabulous. The hotel was amazing and so accommodating. If you ever get the chance to get away, you should go there and visit for a little bit. We decided that we're going to go back on our one-year anniversary next year. So, I hope you can watch Boomer again," I laughed.

"Well, that's wonderful and, yes of course. God willing, I will watch him again. I love this boy," Adriana said as she bent over to kiss Boomer's head.

"Thank you again, Adriana, and here's the little something we brought you back from the Mystic shops, I hope you like it," Tony said as he clipped the leash to Boomer's collar before offering the present.

"Thank you both, I'm sure I'll love it. And congratulations again."

We both hugged her and said our goodbyes. I put Boomer in the back of the truck. Once again, like the perfect gentleman he is, Tony opened my door, kissed me on the cheek, and helped me in. I guess he noticed me tripping up the steps, and just realized he married a total klutz, so he wanted to make sure I didn't fall trying to get into the truck.

Of course, there was one factor I didn't take into consideration. Adriana was half right. I went into this with my heart, but apparently not so much my head. As I heard Boomer settle into the backseat of the truck, my eyes expanded as a name suddenly crossed my mind.

Leah.

"Tony, how are we going to tell Leah? I really don't want her to react negatively about us getting married. And I don't want her to think about stopping me from being Grace's Nanny. You know how much this means to me to be a huge part of Grace's life, and to help raise her in whatever capacity that I can. I feel like I owe this to Nate."

Again, Tony seemed completely collected. *How did he do that? Was that a cop thing?* "Listen, Emma, don't worry about anything; I'll do all the explaining and everything will be fine." His palms gripped the steering wheel. "She needs you to be a part of Grace's life. I mean let's face it, she's not the greatest mother, nor does she show any motherly instincts. I do hate to say that, but I also see that she's not really as caring as she should be towards Grace. Leah is a very selfish person. I stepped in numerous times and said things that I probably shouldn't have, but I need to make sure that Grace is safe."

Just how bad was this situation? As much as I hated Leah, maybe I should have done a little more to be around for Grace.

"Oh my! That's a little unnerving. I am grateful that I am with her during the day, and you are there at night. I think that together we can ensure that she will be okay."

"Yes, Emma, you're right. I think I will tell the realtor to look for a home with a cottage house, or a suite, or something, so Leah can have her own quarters and have a room for Grace as well." Tony seemed to be grasping at straws.

"That's a good idea," I said, feeling somewhat relieved.

We arrived home, unpacked the car, and Tony carried in all the packages and our luggage.

I decided to walk Boomer, he was cooped up in the car for the 45-minute drive home, and I thought he needed to do his business. I told Tony that I was going to walk Boomer down to the cemetery to see Nate. He said to wait up, that he would come with us. I needed time to process a better game plan in regards to Grace. "Hey, Tony, I think I'm going to take Boomer out for a bit. Our usual walk to the cemetery. I'll be back soon."

"No, wait up!" He called out after me. "I'll come."

All the while, I was quiet. Chewing on my lip, I was absorbed in my thoughts. Even Boomer glanced back at me while Tony gave me a gentle nudge. I was a newlywed, I should be worrying about new lingerie for my husband to peel off of me with his teeth. Not the welfare of my baby niece.

Oh well, in a perfect world, it would be the former.

Maybe Nate could shed some light on this. A sign, anything. I spoke out loud to Nate as I always do.

"Hi Nate, it's me and Boomer, and we brought a guest with us today. I'd like you to meet my husband. His name is Tony, and he's a police Lieutenant. He and I got married this weekend and I'm absolutely head over heels in love with him. I wish you were here to meet him, because I know you'd love him, too. Boomer is barking and says hello as he always does when we come to visit you. I'm taking great care of Grace as you can see, and one day I will tell her everything and anything about you. I love you, Nate, and I hope you're happy and safe up in heaven," I said out loud.

I turned to look at Tony who was standing there holding onto Boomer's leash, looking down at Nate's tombstone. He was smiling and saying a silent prayer. It was very touching to see this. I love this man more than I ever imagined loving any man in my life. He's so special to me, he completes me.

"Okay, Tony, let's get going so we can go home and relax. If you're hungry I could put something together for us to eat, then we can settle in and watch a movie."

Boomer barked as if he wanted in on the movie thing. And we both laughed hysterically at the same time. I swear that Boomer is part human, but if I ever said that out loud to anybody, they would probably think I was nuts.

As we proceeded towards the exit, the same lapse of memories came to me. Nate's funeral, seeing Tony for the first time knelt down over Nina's grave. While Tony and Boomer had their own conversation, I grazed over towards where I remembered her place of rest to be. And there it was, the smooth rectangular, angular tombstone aligned with engraved rosettes—permanent flowers likely arranged by Tony.

"Thank you," I whispered to the grave. "Nina, I promise I'll love him forever." As if in response, I felt a faint wisp of breeze caress my cheek. I couldn't help but smile warmly.

When we arrived back, I felt the weight on my shoulders. Rolling along the blades and knotting at the nape of my neck. I reached to the back of my neck as Tony headed into the kitchen. Boomer ran upstairs into the spare room, probably to get his new bone I gave him earlier. Tony and I went to raid the refrigerator to see what we had to eat. He pulled out a bunch of vegetables; squash, orange peppers, red onions, and Yukon potatoes. He said that he was going to make us a roasted vegetable dish that would take about 40-minutes or so in the oven. I thought that sounded delicious since I love vegetables anyway.

The funny thing is, I didn't even know he knew how to cook! I guess I really still have so much more to learn about this man. He told me I should take a seat at the island and that he would take care of everything. I really could get used to this lifestyle. I'm enjoying him and our new life together so much so far.

He put everything in the oven and came over to join me at the kitchen island where I was sitting, and started kissing the side of my neck, which caused goosebumps up my spine. *Well, that was one way to work the knots.*

"You've been quiet since we got back, you okay?" He murmured between kisses. "Now, Mrs. Owens, you know this is unacceptable."

I extended behind me to wrap my arm around his neck.

"Just tired from the trip," I explained. "As much as I like where this is going, why don't we wait until after dinner? We can turn down the bed, snuggle, and watch any movie of your choosing."

Even though we both knew there would be no movie. Which was more than fine by me. I could use a distraction of...sensual proportions. All that would take to light the kindling of my fire would be one kiss. One kiss to draw him into my arms and I'd never let go.

Tony set the table and he lit the candles I had on the table, in the crystal holders my mom had given to me. He remarked how beautiful they were and that warmed my heart. We ate and chatted a little bit about going back to work tomorrow and him telling all the guys he got married. He said they will probably poke fun at his spontaneity, but only because they would never have the nerve to do it themselves, or they would be jealous that he has such a young hot looking wife. I laughed so hard I almost choked on my food.

I cleaned up the dishes because after all, he cooked. I was nearly halfway finished when he snuck up behind me, wrapped his arms around me, and started kissing me again. I can never get enough of this man. I hope he never stops kissing me, surprising me, and holding me the way that he does.

"Mrs. Owens, might I suggest we take this upstairs now?"

"Well, Mr. Owens, I thought you'd never ask," I laughed and ran ahead of him up the stairs.

I tripped once again, and he was right behind me to help me up. We both laughed at my falling again.

"Listen, Emma, you better stop running before you seriously hurt yourself. And this is not a request, it's a demand. I *demand* that you stop running and be more careful. I'm an old man and if I have to worry about you falling all the time, you're going to give me a heart attack. Do you understand? Or do I have to give you a spanking?" He asked teasingly.

You know, I never thought I could get into a man so dominating. But coming from Tony, I think I could live with that.

"Yes, sir," I said coyly, "I need that spanking. But first, you have to catch me."

"I'll not only catch you, but I'm going to spank your bottom until it's bright red. Come here you!"

He grabbed me, picked me up, and put me on the bed. He wiggled my jeans off my hips and flipped me over, all in one swift move. He took his handcuffs off the nightstand and cuffed my hands together above my head. This alone turns me on greatly and he knows this.

He started slapping my butt softly at first, then a little harder. I felt the sting and the burning of it when he slapped for the third time. He spread my legs and entered me roughly and forcibly.

I attempted to make a run for it. I swear I did. But perhaps it was just that Tony was quicker. Because he grabbed me by my waist and picked me up, placing me over his shoulder. Playfully, I beat at his back with my fists in weak attempts to be released. He finally conceded when he tossed me on the bed before situating himself on top of me. While I was trapped beneath him, he reached down and proceeded to tug at the waistband of my jeans and wiggled them off my hips. Panties and all. He flipped me over and took the handcuffs from the nightstand, cuffing my hands skillfully in one quick latch.

My breath hitched at the familiar sound of the handcuffs catching. My excitement pooled in my stomach. Biting my bottom lip, I felt my switch turned on. And like the devil my husband is, he knows exactly how to flip it.

Well, when he said he was going to spank me, he didn't disappoint. Like a dial, he began on *easy,* which I snickered at. Then, to *medium*, where it stung a little harder. I hissed delightfully when he slapped me for a third time, the burning sensation coursing through me and stiffening the peaks of my nipples.

I could hear the ragged breathing of Tony behind me, the excitement stirring inside of him as he chose to show me as much. Spreading my thighs open, at his command, he leaned over behind me and kissed the knot between my shoulders. I exhaled contently before Tony slid into me roughly. I automatically cried out.

"Are you going to be a good girl now and listen to me when I tell you to stop running?" He whispered into my ear, as he pushed his length harder and deeper within me.

I kept wanting more and more.

"No, I won't listen," I moaned.

I needed more.

"Then I will have to spank you more!" Then came another spank.

"No! Oh my God, this feels incredible! Please. Don't. Stop."

"Then tell me what I want to hear, and I'll make you explode," he said in a deep breathy voice.

It was becoming too much. Feeling that gnaw in the pit of my stomach as the coil tightened all over again. Winding me up until I could take no more. Just when I thought I would hit my limit, Tony withdrew, then slammed right back in.

"I will listen and stop running so I don't trip."

"No, tell me you will be a good girl and listen."

"I… am… going to… *ahhh…*" I exploded in total ecstasy. I could no longer hold out.

Shortly after I let go, it was Tony's turn. For the first time since we started having sex, I was no longer worried about getting pregnant. If it happened, then we'd address it. I mean, I adore Grace, and yes, it would be nice to have one of our own. One of the discussions that needed to be had. If I did get pregnant, would it be planned, or pleasantly unexpected? Caring for two babies would be difficult, but with the two of us together, I'm sure we could manage. Tony, after all, seemed more than up for the role of fatherhood once more.

Tony's phone rang and it was almost 2 a.m. When he answered the phone, he seemed quite upset by the conversation. I could hear that it was Leah. She was screaming and carrying on, but I couldn't understand what she was saying. He hung up the phone abruptly and turned to me.

"I'm so sorry, Emma. I have to go," said Tony as he jumped up and quickly put on his jeans. The speed in which he was pacing himself had me worried, as the post-coital glow was instead replaced by an adrenaline rush.

"What's wrong?" I asked worriedly.

Tony's brows knitted together, the firm zip of his jacket caused me to flinch. "Don't worry, Emma, I'll take care of it. I'll talk to you when I get back. I have to go right now. I don't have time to explain."

"Tony, is everything okay? Please don't leave me like this."

"Everything will be okay; I just need to take care of something. I'll be right back, I love you," he said as he kissed me quickly on the lips, and out the door he went.

I really couldn't imagine what had just happened with Leah. I suddenly became very worried about Grace, praying that she was alright. I knew Tony would never let anything happen to her. She means the world to me and he knows that.

I couldn't sleep so I went downstairs to make a cup of chamomile honey and vanilla tea. Boomer came running after me. I sat at the kitchen island with Boomer at my feet, sipping my tea waiting for Tony to come back.

Dear Journal,

We picked Boomer up from Adriana—a woman I want to get together with more often. She's so sweet and so important to me. I don't know what my life would be like without her, as all of my friends hold such special places in my heart.

Well, we made our first decision as a married couple. We decided to put both of our houses on the market to invest in one of our own.

Something creeping in the back of my mind, that as much as Tony had tried to assure me...I don't know, Journal. I just can't seem to ease myself out of it. Maybe I should have been smarter, or we should have had a talk about the use of protection. It could be possible that I'm pregnant. I'm 35-years-old...I've grown up understanding that at 35, it gets harder to conceive as I age.

But I will cross that bridge when I come to it.

Caden had texted me, but I was too distracted with the newness of my new husband. Actually, the man's kind of kinky. He really loves to play with his cuffs, and I wonder just how much action they get outside of the bedroom.

Not to say I'm disappointed...trust me, I'm not.

~Emma

Till Death Do Us Part

~Chapter 14~

The Green-Eyed Monster

It was two long hours before Tony came back. I was worried sick about what was happening at his home with Grace and Leah. I ran to the door and opened it quickly, to find Tony standing there with Grace in his arms.

"Hi, Emma. Please take Grace, I need to get her things from my truck," he said.

I didn't say a word, I just took Grace into my arms and held her tight. I looked down at her and it seemed almost as if she was trying to smile at me. She was three months old now, and although I really didn't know everything about babies, I figured that she probably just released gas or something and that was what the smile was about. I gave her a big kiss on her full rosy-colored cheek, and she cooed back at me. Well, I guess she liked that kiss from her Auntie Emma.

Tony carried in Grace's portable crib, a small suitcase, a box of diapers, and a case of formula. I was surprised by all of this. All I could think of was that Grace was going to be spending the night. But did she really need all this stuff?

"Emma, I'll set up the crib in the spare room if that's okay. And then I'll explain what just happened."

"Yes, Tony, of course. I think Grace went potty, so I will change her."

"Thanks, Emma. We will talk when I get back down here."

I changed her diaper and I made her a bottle of warm formula. I sat down on my sofa to feed her. She finished half the bottle and fell asleep in my arms. I burped her and then Tony came down and took her from my arms and brought her upstairs and put her in her crib.

When he came back down, I noticed this scowl that was across his face. Gone was the happy smile he usually carried around.

"Tony, what's wrong? You looked worried."

"Emma, when Leah called me earlier, she was carrying on something fierce. She was saying crazy things like she didn't want Grace anymore, that Grace was cramping her style, and crazy things like that. I was afraid she may hurt Grace, that's why I ran over there. When I got there, Grace was sleeping in her crib and she was safe."

I knew Leah was a terrible person, but I didn't think she was capable of this.

"Oh my God! Tony, how are we going to keep Grace safe?" I said as the tears poured down my cheeks.

"All I could think of doing, for now, was to take Grace here and leave her with us," he said holding my hand, "Leah seemed pleased that I was taking her. The whole situation was so surreal. I couldn't believe how she was acting."

"Do you think she would have hurt her?"

"No, I don't. But my instincts told me to take her. And Leah let me without putting up a fuss."

Is she serious? I wish Leah was in front of me right now. There was only one word for her: unfit.

"Tony," I began, trying to keep calm, "What will we do now?"

"She doesn't know where you live, so Grace is safe. I will take a leave of absence from work and we can figure this whole thing out. I'll go see my Sargent later today. Let's get some sleep. Things always look better in the morning."

I couldn't even wrap my head around all of this. Leah didn't want her baby. Where would that leave Grace? I needed to protect her as best as I could. I promised Nate I would always be there for her.

Grace was my flesh and blood. Even though I didn't birth Grace, she was every bit of mine.

With this thought in my head, I tossed and turned, and finally fell asleep when my alarm went off. A sleepless night well spent in regard to attempting to formulate a plan to keep my baby niece safe. I rubbed the back of my neck and walked into the kitchen to find that Tony was already up and feeding Grace. He managed to make a pot of tea, too.

"Hey you," he said as he kissed my head.

My eyes fell upon the small head of Grace. That baby meant more to me than anyone could fathom. Possibly even Nate, who I had a feeling dipped his hands into my fate. Thoughts of potential pregnancy pushed aside, all I could think about was saving Grace. Call it maternal instincts kicking in. Where were Leah's? "Good morning to the two loves of my life."

"Emma, I have been thinking long and hard about this since last night. Firstly, I called my Sargent and I told him he needed a week off. He granted it to me, no questions asked. Secondly, I called Leah and told her I needed to come home and talk to her. She said she would wait for me before going to work. I made you white pomegranate tea, and Grace is fed, changed, and ready for her morning nap. I'll go talk to Leah and see if we can sort this thing out."

Let's hope that fate was on our side. Hopefully Tony could manage to make a deal that wouldn't set Leah off. I couldn't tell at this point what she was capable of if she was acting this unstable. I prayed for him for the best of luck. It truly was a conquest.

"Okay, Tony. I'll bring her up to her crib. I love you, and good luck," I said as I kissed him goodbye.

I couldn't believe what was going on here. Leah gave birth to Nate's baby, my niece, and now she wanted no part of her.

I just don't get it. I know Tony said she was selfish but didn't she want Grace? And wasn't it instinctive to put her baby first?

My head was spinning with all these thoughts of Tony and I raising Grace and getting Leah out of the picture.

The question still remained—how?

At that moment, my cell rang and it was Caden. I could see from the caller ID.

"Hello, Caden. How are you?" I asked as cheerfully as I could.

"I'm great, Em. How are you?"

"Well, there is so much to tell you. Are you sitting down, Caden? And do you have the time to chat?"

"Well, yes I am. But how about we meet for tea in like an hour?"

"I have a better idea. Do you want to come here? I can't get away right now, and this would be easier for me."

"Yeah, sure. I'll see you soon," he said and hung up.

I had a few minutes to wash up, straighten the house, and check on Grace. I peeked into the room and she was sleeping soundly. She tends to take long naps which is good, so I will have time to get things done.

I returned to the kitchen when I was dressed, I made a fresh pot of tea and took out a roll of Pillsbury cookies. I figured these are easy to make and that they would only take a few minutes to bake. I know that Caden would like them with his tea.

I heard Caden pull up in the driveway as soon as I took the cookies out of the oven.

"Perfect timing," I said out loud.

Leaving the cookies to cool, I shut the oven off and hurried to the door. Opening it, I saw Caden's green eyes gaze up at me with a sparkle in them, more than happy to see me after so long. The same gaze I used to get years ago that I thought had dimmed away.

"Hello, Caden," I said as I kissed his cheek, "Come on in. I just made fresh tea and I baked some cookies to go with it."

He rubbed his hands together eagerly before collecting me in a surprising embrace. "Nice, thanks Em, you're spoiling me."

I squeezed him before letting him go, guiding him through the hall and into the kitchen to sit at the table. "Sure, anytime. So, tell me Caden what have you been up to?"

"Well, I got back from London last week when I had called you. I wanted to see how it was going with you working for Leah, and if she recognized you when she saw you." His eyes followed me as I grabbed the tea kettle, two mugs dangling from my fingers by their handles. "By the way Em, you look amazing. You don't look like Nate's little sister, anymore. Something has changed for you, what is it?"

I felt my cheeks redden, "Actually, Caden, a lot has changed," I said, as I held up my wedding band finger to show him.

His face dropped entirely, catching himself as he began to stammer, "Wait, what? You got married? When? Who? I've only been gone ten months. I didn't even know you were seriously dating anyone."

"It's a long story," I quickly explained.

Caden leaned back in his seat, taking one of the prepared mugs and raised his mug of peppermint tea up at me, "And I've got the time to kill. I want to hear every detail."

I began with how I met Tony at Nate's funeral unexpectedly. Then I proceeded to take him through that creep, Adam, and how Tony was there at every turn.

"Every turn?" Caden asked suspiciously. "Are you sure *he* isn't the stalker?"

"Caden!" I admonished, "That stalker is my husband."

He held his hands up in defense, "Kidding, Em. Kidding! Don't you remember my tenth-grade girlfriend? Stalker material."

I gave him a look and continued by explaining Leah, Grace, working for Leah, and her outrageous behavior.

"Leah was so erratic, a real wildcard, I couldn't keep up with her and her flashy lifestyle she wanted to maintain," I found myself rambling, "I mean, did it ever occur to her that that comes to an end when you have a baby? Did she miss the message? The only person who suffers here is Grace. She deserves a mother and not a flyby nightmare."

"So, you mean Grace is here now?" Caden turned his head up in the direction of the nursery. I saw his face change, all of his playfulness had vanished. It hadn't occurred to me until now that Caden likely had never seen Grace or how she looks so much like her father.

Thank God she looks nearly identical to Nate.

"Listen, Em. I came here for another reason. Don't get me wrong, I really wanted to see you. I always want to see you."

Now I was concerned.

"Caden? What's wrong?" My lips shifted into a frown. I took my place back at the table, scooching my chair closer to his. Caden seemed to waste no time as he reached out to grab my available hand.

"Em, listen, I never had a chance to tell you before. I didn't want to break up how happy you've been. But I won't lie to you, I've been struggling with Nate's death." His emerald eyes dropped to the table as he swallowed hard, trying to weigh the thickness down as I took note of how choked his voice became.

In turn, I squeezed his hand and leaned in close. "Listen, I miss him, too. Don't you think it pains me that I see him every time I look into Grace's eyes?"

Tears pricked the corners of his eyes. "That's not it. While I was in Milan, it had me thinking. I lost Nate, I can't lose you, too."

My eyes widened as I leaned back, "Caden, you're never going to lose me." I barely heard the front door open and close. "We've always been in this together. And we'll get through it the same way."

"That's not what I mean," he said. His eyes searched mine, hoping I would catch what he was trying to say without him outright saying it. A chill coursed through me as I shivered.

"Then...what do you mean?"

"Emma?" Came the voice of Tony.

I jerked upright, quickly snatching my hand from Caden's grasp, "In the kitchen, Tony."

He walked right over to me and kissed me hard on the lips in a very possessive way. That was a little surprising.

Oh...did he hear?

I had to act natural, "Tony, I'd like you to meet Caden. He was my brother's best friend. We've known each other since high school."

"Hey, Caden, nice to meet you," said Tony as he firmly grasped and squeezed Caden's hand while he was shaking it.

Caden looked at a cross between shocked and disturbed. "Um, yeah nice to meet you too," said Caden, as he looked up at me. "Em, I'm gonna get going. I need to do some work. I'll text you later."

"Yes, okay, Caden, I'll walk you out."

As I was walking him to the door, Tony followed me, but he didn't come outside with us. I walked over to Caden's car where I kissed him on the cheek and hugged him. He got into his car and drove off.

I came back into the house to see Tony watching us out from the front window.

"Spying on me, Tony?"

"No, not really. You've never mentioned that you were so chummy with Caden."

"Tony, are you *jealous?* You have no reason to be, really. He and I go way back, he was Nate's best friend. I told you about him."

Tony crossed his arms over his chest. "No, I'm not jealous. I'm just always suspicious of people I don't know. It's a perk of the job, I guess."

I could feel his anger as I tried to soothe him. Between Caden's heartfelt statement and my husband's jealousy, I wasn't sure how to handle it. "Tony, look, I love you and only you. You please me in every way, I have no desire to be with any other man. Okay?"

He was like a human lie detector. Sensing my sincerity in my words, his shoulders lowered. "Yes, Emma, I'm sorry. It was just that I came home and saw you talking to this good-looking young guy and I was just... well you know... I guess I was a *little* jealous."

"No need to be ever. No matter what guy I talk to. I have a good idea, let's go upstairs and I'll show you just how much I want and desire only you. Grace isn't due to wake up for another hour or so." I took off running and Tony yelled for me to stop and I did, he was right, I may fall and hurt myself one day.

We made love hard and furiously, and I didn't want it to end. But all of a sudden, we heard Grace let out a loud wail.

"Uh-oh, I think someone wants to eat," said Tony.

"Well her timing couldn't be better, Grandpa."

"Hmm, about that grandpa thing, how would you feel if we became Grace's parents?"

Again, we're syncing minds.

"What? Tony, wait a minute, let me get Grace and feed her. We can talk afterwards," I jumped up and put on my long t-shirt and went to get Grace.

I sat at the kitchen feeding her when Tony came in and explained that Leah wanted to give up Grace for adoption. Leah felt she couldn't handle raising a baby alone. She knew she would always be alone because Nate was gone. She also felt it was a financial burden and that no guys would want to date a girl that was tied down with a child.

I suppose it would be a difficult situation for her. However, I can't feel that bad for the slut.

Tony and I decided that if Leah was being truthful about her feelings, then we would adopt Grace and raise her as our own. Tony also explained to Leah that he and I had gotten married this weekend while we were away. She was surprised but didn't seem to care very much. She told Tony that she thought I was great with Grace and that I would make her a very good mother.

The first smart thing she has said in the history of ever.

The next couple of days came and went rather quickly. Tony had a lot of connections in law enforcement and had all the paperwork expedited for Grace's adoption. Leah signed it and never looked back. She packed her things and told Tony she was moving, that night, to Las Vegas with a friend. He asked her if she wanted to say goodbye to Grace and she told him he could do it for her. Leah didn't seem to have any motherly instincts whatsoever. And that was fine, for Grace was now ours.

I couldn't believe how we became sudden parents to Grace. I swore that Nate had his hand in this, somehow. I went from being unmarried a couple of weeks ago, to going on vacation, coming home married, and less than a week later I became an immediate mother to my niece.

Life. Was. Good.

Oh my God, Journal!

If I thought I hated Leah before when she was with Nate, she's absolutely no better with his daughter. Tony had left late in the night to rescue Grace from her. She's selfish, she's immature, unfit to be a mother, and the list goes on...

I'm sorry, I'm not a hateful person. I hate to carry hate in my heart, but I think this can be an exception.

Grace is better off with us. And I don't care what it takes, I'm not giving her up. Try to pry her from my arms.

In other news, while Grace was asleep, Caden had stopped by. He seemed surprised and taken aback that I had eloped with a man I barely knew. Caden couldn't seem to understand how the heart wants what it wants, and I'm not saying I disagreed with his logic. But you know what? My life is my own to lead.

However, Tony's green-eyed monster reared its head again. I wonder if this will be a recurring thing. While I'm starting to get the idea of how Caden really feels, he still is an important factor in my life, as well as Grace's. He is every bit of an uncle to her.

Tony needs to understand that not every younger guy is a threat. I wish he could see clearly that I chose him above all the younger guys for a reason. Plain and simple, I love him. Or is that not enough?

~Emma

Till Death Do Us Part

~Chapter 15~

The New Addition

"Carole! Hey, Anthony Owens. Listen, I need my house put up on the market as soon as you can. Think it can happen?" Tony asked. With Leah being gone and moved out, Tony hardly had a reason to keep that house with all of the negative memories attached to it. "Yeah, that's right. Priced to sell. As soon as you can make it happen. Uh-huh, thanks, Carole."

While I indulged myself with Grace reaching to hold the bottle on her own, my eyes picked up to watch Tony pace the room while he was on the phone with Carole.

"How'd it go?" I asked, shifting the bottle onto the coffee table once Grace was through. She was such a good baby.

"Carole says that the house is beautiful, it should sell quickly. She has no doubts about it." He tapped his phone against his hand as he looked up towards the ceiling.

Not that I doubted Carole. I'm sure she was right. "Well, then I wouldn't stock too much into it. If Carole can work her magic, then she'll make it happen."

Carole was right! Within two weeks' time, he had two very nice offers on the house. One a little higher than the other. He told Carole that he would take the highest offer and to let him know when she could set up a time and place to sign the paperwork.

While all this was going on, we had settled into a nice routine with Grace. I had gotten her on a schedule, and she would follow it almost to the minute. She was growing into a nice, happy little person. It was during this time that I noticed that I was super tired, more than I usually am. Tony blamed it on the fact that we have had so much going on and we were constantly running around doing things. He said I just needed to rest. But for some reason, I felt it was something more. I decided to make an appointment with my doctor for the following day. I figured I'd take my chances and see if she was available, and I was so fortunate that she was. I asked Tony to come home a little earlier tomorrow night so I could have him watch Grace and I could go see my doctor. So, he did just that.

I went to see Dr. Hart. She is my primary doctor and my gynecologist. I sat at the table, my feet toying with the stirrups while I waited. All around the room were much of what a person would normally see in a gynecologist's office, plastic figures, posters--purple silhouette figures of women in the varying stages of pregnancy, even copies of *What to Expect When You're Expecting.*

"Hello, Emma. How have you been? Tell me what's going on," Dr. Hart said as she entered the room.

"I'm good. Just a little tired lately. My new husband and I adopted a baby. So, I was thinking because I'm getting less sleep, due to her waking up in the middle of the night for a feeding, that's why I've been so tired." I even sounded tired. Dr. Hart offered a sympathetic smile and continued on with her questionnaire.

"That could be, Emma. Have you been nauseous or anything?"

"Yes, sometimes when I get up in the morning."

"Okay, Emma, I'm going to have you urinate in a cup, and then we will do some blood work. My assistant will be in with you shortly. Stay put," she said as she walked out the door.

A young girl walked into the examination room, carrying a tray of needles and the sample cups. Immediately, I felt my stomach lurch from nerves. I really don't like needles.

"Hi, Emma, you are going to feel a little pinch. If you want, just turn your head and look the other way as I take your blood," she said.

"Okay, I will. Thanks."

It was over faster than I thought. She told me to take the cup, urinate in it, and leave it in the bathroom. Following that, a lab tech would take it and test it.

Dr. Hart came in about 15-minutes later and said she knew exactly what was causing my fatigue and nausea.

She was trying her utmost to keep a professional poker face, but I could see her trying to fight a smile. "Emma, I have some news for you. You are about six weeks pregnant. Congratulations."

Wait, what? Seriously?

"I'm...what? I'm pregnant?"

"Why yes, six weeks," Dr. Hart calmly responded. "Everything came back smoothly. Are you surprised?"

"Yes, I....um, I mean no. My husband and I weren't actively trying. I always knew there was a possibility." I recalled the conversations vividly, Tony's assurances. "I just assumed that women at my age would have a harder time…"

Dr. Hart appeared nothing but understanding. "Emma, years ago, women were having babies at much younger ages, that's true. It's pretty common nowadays for older women to have perfectly normal pregnancies. As long as you're healthy, I don't see why that can't be so. Besides, I'll be there every step of the way. We'll do any and all tests you're comfortable with to make sure the baby is as perfect as can be."

She calmed my concerns, quelled my fears, and left me feeling a little bit better. It was perfectly normal, she said. All I could do was nod in response, my mind reeling with the fact that there was a combination of Tony and I inside of me. Proof of our love for one another.

"Since you're six weeks, I'd like to take a peek with an ultrasound."

Oh, I wish Tony were here to see this. But I was quickly devising a plan to surprise him. Dr. Hart gave me a moment to prepare myself by undressing from the waist down and lay a sheet over myself, putting my feet on the stirrups. When she returned, she began prepping a wand-like device.

"Since you're so early in your pregnancy, we're going to conduct a transvaginal ultrasound. Just want to make sure everything's good, see if we can catch the heartbeat, and get you a picture of your baby."

She told me to breathe, and I did. I adjusted myself before Dr. Hart's hand disappeared beneath the sheet. I didn't feel much aside from a mild bout of pressure.

"Looking good. Not ectopic, which is good," she murmured. I closed my eyes with relief before turning my head over to the screen. Dr. Hart explained where everything was, pointing to the small bean in the center. My breath practically left me. Dr. Hart pressed a button, the room suddenly filled with the rush of a sound, erratic beating of...a heart.

"My favorite part about the job," Dr. Hart said. "This moment." I turned to Dr. Hart, tears bubbling and slipping down the corners of my eyes as they resumed their gluing to the screen. My baby, growing, its little heart telling me everything's okay.

For the most part, I was speechless. Lost in the glow of new motherhood. Dr. Hart scheduled me for my second ultrasound, one that would better determine the baby's gender. This one, she wanted me to bring Tony along. I have no doubts he'd want to be present.

She put together a collected care package. One that included my prescription for prenatal vitamins, pamphlets, and other reading material. She gifted me her copy of *What to Expect*, along with the greatest gift of all—my baby's first picture.

Dr. Hart shook my hand and walked out after setting me up and giving me a congratulatory hug. I put on my shoes and left the doctor's office as if I was floating on air. *I'm pregnant... I'm going to have a baby... Grace is going to have a sister or brother... none of this was sinking in just yet. Wait till I tell Tony!*

I came home and Tony was feeding Grace, she seemed a little irritable this morning for some reason. I told Tony that she was probably not sleeping well in the porta-crib anymore. She was growing at a rapid rate and needed a full-sized crib now. I told him we needed to go shopping for all her necessities this weekend. This was, after all, going to be her new home now.

"Hi, honey. I need to talk to you about my doctor's visit. I have some news…" I said cautiously.

"Emma, what is it? You know you can tell me anything, don't you?"

"Yes, Tony of course I do. It's actually really good news. I'm pregnant."

He didn't say a word at first, he carefully placed Grace in her little swing. Then he turned around swiftly, grabbed me in his arms, and picked me up off the floor. He hugged and kissed me so hard. He placed me back on the floor again and dropped to one knee in front of me, placing both hands on my belly and he started talking to it.

"Hello in there, little one. Mommy and Daddy love you and want you so much. We can't wait for you to come meet your big sister, Grace," he said with tears in his eyes.

I placed a hand on each side of his face, I lifted his head so I could see his eyes, "Tony, I don't think I could love you any more than I do right now."

"I love you, Emma. And thank you for this gift you have given me. Our family is now complete. You have made me the happiest man alive."

"Aww, Tony, now you have me crying too," I said as I got down on the floor to hug him again. I reached for my purse that had fallen, withdrawing the envelope that contained our baby's picture. I handed it over to Tony without saying a word.

He looked at me, perplexed before leaning back to sit upon his heels and open it. Carefully, he slid out the photo and stared in awe. He gazed at the image for a good few minutes before collecting me back into his arms with a wide smile.

"Emma, you don't understand, I never thought I'd get married, much less have two children. I can't tell you how happy you have made me. I will live my life making sure you and our girls never want for anything."

"*Girls?* How do you know our baby will be a girl?" I laughed uncontrollably.

He feigned offense. "I kind of know things, Emma. Trust me, she's a girl."

"Wow, okay. That would be wonderful if Grace had a sister. They would be close in age which would be great for the two of them."

"Yes, Emma, I agree." He paused. "Oh wait, we need to come up with a name for her. How do you like the name, Ava?"

Now I was wondering if he had this name stored in his back pocket. But, admittedly, I did like it.

"I love the name, Ava. Can we give her the name Elizabeth as her middle name? It was my mom's name."

"Well, when why don't we name her Ava-Elizabeth? Use both names as her first name, I think it would be really special."

I was so touched. I couldn't agree more.

On that note, Grace woke up wailing away. Tony reacted and picked her up immediately. I suggested we go for a walk with her and Boomer after lunch. I wanted to keep my weight in check now that I was pregnant, and after working so hard to lose weight, I didn't want to gain it all back and not be in shape again.

I made us lunch as he changed Grace's diaper and got a bottle ready for her midday feeding at noon. She was on a wonderful schedule now and I hoped to keep her that way to make things easier for me when our new baby arrived.

I loved that Tony is a hands-on dad, never being told to go feed the baby or anything. It was like a natural thing to him. He was already the perfect father and the perfect husband.

I never thought I'd have any children and here I am having two babies. I truly feel so blessed.

Tony sat at the island after feeding Grace and placed her in her swing. We decided that we needed to get rolling and make my spare room in the house the girls' room.

Look at me, he now has me convinced the baby is a girl. How could he possibly know?

I know he has great instincts, but to know this is a girl… wow… that borders being a sensitive psychic, or intuitive. Maybe he is and he doesn't want to tell me yet. I'll have to ask him when we go for our walk.

I made us sandwiches and for some reason, I wanted pickles on mine. What a weird choice I thought to myself. And Tony laughed out loud as he watched me put the pickles on my ham and swiss cheese sandwich.

"You know, Emma, that really is gross," he laughed.

"No, it's delicious. You need to try it." I held it up towards him. "Here, have a bite."

He stepped back as he chuckled. "Oh no, I'll pass, thanks."

We both couldn't stop laughing and we ended up waking up Grace from laughing so loud. I picked her up and put on her little sweater and grabbed her blanket. Tony got Boomer's leash and hooked it on his collar. We were all set for our walk. I figured I could clean up the dishes later.

I decided we should walk as I always did, down to the cemetery to visit with Nate. I needed to tell him the great news.

"Okay, I have to ask, because I know there is a story in there somewhere. How do you know Ava-Elizabeth is a girl?" I asked.

He glanced at me, appearing hesitant to answer. Intuition was always a sensitive subject, especially when it couldn't be explained. "I always knew I had the gift of knowing or seeing things before they happened. My dear grandmother, Clara, had the gift as well. I was afraid of it as a child. But as a cop, I have used it many times, and it has helped me to save lives. No one at the force knows I have this gift. They just assume I'm a well-seasoned cop. Do you believe in this kind of thing Emma?"

See, here's the thing--we've both had paranormal influences in our lives. Another connective point that brought us together.

"Yes, I do, in fact, I have the gift as well. But I have never used it, and probably lost it."

Before I even realized it, we were at the cemetery almost in front of Nate. I guess I must be in better shape these days from all the walking I do because the walk seemed faster and easier.

I walked up to Nate's tombstone and placed a pretty shiny rock on it that I had found by my house. They say you should always place a rock on the tombstone, for it shows that person had been visited by a loved one.

"Hey Nate, I have some good news for you," I said out loud while looking up at the sky, "Grace is our daughter now. I know you had a hand in this, and I wanted to say thank you. I promise to raise Grace like she is ours. I will also keep your memory alive for her when she is old enough to understand. And Nate, *I'm pregnant.* Tony swears it's a girl. I really hope so, too, for I think she will be a wonderful playmate for Grace. I love and miss you, Nate, and wish you were here to share in all the good things happening in my life right now. I know you are in my heart and will always be there. God bless you, Nate."

Tony bowed his head as I spoke to my brother. He said he also believed that Nate could hear me and that he had helped us to get Grace. He knew Grace would be in danger with Leah. And what a shame that her biological birth mother is irresponsible and immature. Besides she's too much of a party-girl. That's not a good life for a child to be exposed to. I would never let that happen! An unstable wildcard.

I firmly believe that all things happen for a reason. And it occurred to me that it was meant for Leah to have Grace so that I could raise her.

Oh my God, Journal!

I don't believe it. I mean, I should. So much has transpired. Leah outright gave up her rights to Grace. Tony called about listing his home with his realtor friend, Carole, who assured us that his home would sell both quickly and for a nice penny. This assured Tony because he explained to me that it would establish a nest egg in the event something happened to him. That myself and Grace would be well taken care of.

I wish he wouldn't talk like that. As much as I accept the reality of marrying a Lieutenant and the high risk that comes with the title, I just...would rather not.

Especially because I found out I'm pregnant. Dr. Hart and I met little Ava-Elizabeth as a bean on a screen. I heard her heartbeat and it was the most incredible thing I've heard since Tony told me that he loved me.

~Emma

~Chapter 16~

Till Death Do Us Part

Days run into weeks that run into months and time seems to go by so fast. Grace is almost nine months old now, and she's crawling all over the house and getting into all sorts of trouble. She steals Boomer's bones and tries to eat them. Boomer is so patient, and he gently retrieves his bones from her. He loves her and protects her, too.

I'm seven months pregnant now and feeling more exhausted than ever. I do suppose it's more likely that chasing Grace around is tiring me out, but the pregnancy is just as draining. I feel good mostly, except for the tiredness. I walk almost every day and that helps to keep me fit. Dr. Hart says the baby is growing well.

The baby was also confirmed to be a girl.

Tony has been a wonderful help; he comes home from work a little earlier each day. He jumps right in and takes care of Grace while I prepare dinner. Some days, he even cooks for us and tells me to take a nap while he does it. He is the most amazing husband and father. I believe in my heart that everything happens for a reason. Seeing him everywhere I went but not knowing him at that time was meant to be. Having that psycho break into my home was, I hate to say it, meant to be, because that's when Tony and I started dating. That situation had brought us together.

Tony left for work a little earlier than usual today, he said he needed to do a ton of paperwork on this case he was working on. He always kisses me goodbye and tells me he loves me before he leaves. It's a nice routine we have gotten into. We always say *I love you* before we go to bed, too, even if we had an argument that day. We never stay mad at each other for long and we definitely don't go to bed angry, not ever.

I had to stop working my virtual assistant job, I just don't have the time anymore to do it. Between Grace, the housework, Tony, my pregnancy, Boomer, and everything else in a day that I take care of--it became impossible for me to work. Tony had told me to quit, he made more than enough income to take care of all of us and the house. Besides, his home sold for a pretty penny and now we had that money in savings too.

We decided not to sell my home, because it was perfect for all of us and my mortgage would be paid off in five short years and we would own the house outright. We figured this would make more sense financially. Tony did want to finish the basement and make a den or playroom down there, and an office. I thought this was a great idea and when the girls got older, they could hang out at home with their friends. It was a safer place to be, than having them hang out on the street and possibly get into trouble.

Caden and Tony had made amends. Both of the men connected to me were important to me and they both realized that. When I had explained to Tony that it meant the world to Caden to part of Grace's life, I could tell that Tony understood a little better. It wasn't just for me, it was for Nate, too.

After our last meeting, and the announcement of my marriage to Tony, Caden soon started dating someone else. And something tells me that puts Tony's mind at ease.

We asked Caden to be Graces' godfather and we had a small intimate ceremony in the church with Father Layhe. Caden was so happy we had chosen him, and he vowed to always look out for Grace. Caden was a big part of our lives and he adored babysitting for Grace when we needed to attend functions for Tony's job.

I was certain that Caden would marry that girl. He eventually proposed to her in Milan, where they met. He told me they kept in contact and she was really interested in him. I mean, sure, why wouldn't she? She had even come to the states in pursuit of him. I told him to go for it, and he did.

But something wasn't right. Caden called the engagement off. Something about her not being the love of his life, and he couldn't marry someone who wasn't.

He and I became closer as time progressed. As close as he and Nate were. Caden would sometimes accompany Grace and I on walks to see Nate, but it made him feel too sad, and he slowly stopped coming. However, he did start taking Boomer on walks, just like Nate did, and Boomer loved it.

Today, he was coming over for tea and to catch up. But I think he was more so coming over for Grace. She was the girl of the hour, the apple of his eye.

I was so lost in my thoughts; I didn't hear the doorbell ring until Boomer started barking and running towards the front door. It was Caden stopping by before he left again for Italy.

"Hi, Caden, come in, the coffee's ready," I said as I opened the door and kissed him hello.

"Hey, Boomer. Hi, Em, where is my little princess?"

"Your princess is in for her morning nap. She should be up soon. So, tell me Caden, where in Italy are you going now?"

"I'm going back to Milan, actually. There is this big show I need to see and all the new clothing lines for next year will be available for purchase. I'm really looking forward to it. Even though it's work, I do get to have fun too."

"Wow, you lead this amazing life as a fashion designer. I always thought of studying design when I was in college, and then I changed my mind."

"It's never too late to follow your dreams, Em. I mean you'd have to wait till the girls are in school and then you could go back. Ya know? Did Danny and Sandy give up on one another? Or did Frenchie give up after beauty school was a bust?"

"Yeah, I suppose I could. But I'll be an old lady by that time!"

"Old? You? Never! You will always be young at heart."

Caden hugged me tightly as he said it. I hugged him back. I love this guy. He's so positive and so good to all of us.

We continued to chat and then my doorbell rang again. I wasn't expecting anyone, so Caden said he would get it. In the background, I had the news on. I usually don't, because the news was too depressing. More negativity in the world than positive. Not that I lived in a bubble. Something told me to have it turned on. A reporter was covering a headlining story.

Though, I couldn't focus on the reporter. I was more concentrated on Caden at my front door. I heard him whispering to someone, so I decided to see what that was all about.

"Em, I think you need to sit down," said Caden.

"...Police Lieutenant was shot and killed at the scene."

My blood ran cold. Why was Johnson here and not my husband? I knew how this went, but I didn't want to admit it. "What's going on, why are you here Detective Johnson?" I felt my voice raise. "Where's Tony? Tell me! What is going on, I asked you." It was climbing to levels of hysteria.

"Emma, please sit down," said Caden.

Detective Johnson started to speak, "Emma, I'm so sorry, it's Tony. He... he was fatally injured in the line of duty."

"Locals say he was responding to an incident at a local single's meet, the Pork & Rind. *Manager John Elmond stated a disgruntled former employee had broken in before hours. He had a concealed weapon on his person."*

"He was what? You aren't making any sense, there must be a mistake! I'm pregnant with his baby! Can't you see that? I spoke to him on his way to work. Oh my God! I just don't understand."

"Emma, you need to sit down, please," said Caden as he ushered me into the chair in the living room.

"None of this makes any sense, Caden," I said, as the tears poured from my eyes and stained the front of my blouse.

Johnson came in, sat down, and held my hands, "Emma, I was with him when he died. I was the first person on the scene when the call came in, he wasn't alone. I'm so sorry."

"*No! It can't be!* I'm having Ava-Elizabeth in a couple of months; he needs to be here for his daughter. This. Can't. Be. Happening. Oh my God, help me!"

The room started spinning and Caden's voice started fading. His face was becoming blurry and then everything went black.

I could hear the faint echo from the television confirm my worst nightmares, *"The records confirm that the lieutenant was identified as Anthony Owens. He was 55."*

"Emma? Emma, can you hear me? I am EMT Desiree Martinez, we are going to transport you to the hospital now. You and your baby will be fine."

"Grace... Where's Grace?"

"Em, I have her and will stay with her. Don't worry she'll be fine," said Caden as he kissed my head.

I nodded again and closed my eyes. *This can't be happening*, I said to myself. How could Tony be gone? Ava-Elizabeth is due to arrive in two months. What will I do without him? How can I raise two babies alone?

I woke up in the hospital, not remembering much of what happened. The resident doctor came in to explain to me what was going on. He told me that I passed out at home after hearing the devastating news about my husband.

The loud hysterical sobs, I did not recognize were my own. One would think the sounds they heard were from an animal being savagely beaten and torn apart by a beast larger than its being. I couldn't control myself. I felt as though my breath was stuck in my throat as it was closing, making it harder to breathe.

"Emma, I am going to give you a little oxygen. You need to calm yourself and take deep breaths. Do it for your babies," said the doctor. I didn't even know his name.

I fell asleep again and woke up to Caden holding my hand and sitting in a seat next to the bed.

"Caden... he's gone," I could barely speak as I said it, my throat was raw and my voice almost nonexistent, "first Nate, and now Tony."

"I know, Em. I will always be here to help you with Grace and Ava. Don't worry about that, I won't let you raise them alone."

"Caden... thank you," I whispered.

"Emma, please try to rest and don't worry about Grace. You need to take care of you and Ava-Elizabeth right now. Okay? Promise me you will work on that. The doctor said you can come home in a day or two. They want to make sure you are hydrated and feeling stronger. They also want to make sure that Ava is doing well," explained Caden.

"I will, Caden. I hate hospitals and I want to get home to Grace, and to you, too."

Caden was a great friend, and I loved him dearly. I know he loved me, too. I thank God that he is in our lives, for he is all we have left now.

Journal…

Caden just left the room. As grateful as I am that he's here, he's not the one I want in the room with me. I'm months away from giving birth to Ava-Elizabeth and my husband is dead.

DEAD.

I feel like a part of me has just been torn out. I want to find out who did this to him. I want to inflict on them what they did to Tony. And while I shouldn't be mad at him-- Tony, how could you leave us? HOW!?

~Emma

Till Death Do Us Part

~Chapter 17~

The Lost Love

All is quiet in St. Charles Cemetery, once again, as it should be.

Father Layhe stands at the end of a royal blue coffin, beside an enlarged framed picture of Tony smiling, encompassed by flowers. How people would want him to be remembered. I had decided it would be best if he was buried next to Nina. Even in death, I could never look to slight her.

I didn't think I would be doing this again, not so soon. Ava would come into this world in the same way that Grace was to be raised, on the memories of their fathers.

More than half the police force attended, along with Suzie, and other friends of Tony.

This time, Leah was nowhere to be found. No giggling misinterpretations between her and Caden, who I know had tried to reach out to her. Her phone was no longer in service, and perhaps that was for the best.

At my side with his arm wrapped around me is Caden. Supporting me upright as the weight of my grief and pregnancy were taking their vicious tolls. He had Grace upon his hip in the opposite hand. Ava moved around inside of me as uncomfortably as I felt. Likely looking for any remainder of space that she could muster.

Father Layhe turned his head to survey the group of us before beginning, "Today, friends, we honor a loving husband and father, Lieutenant Anthony Owens. Departed from this world, way too soon, but not from the hearts of those who loved him. Emma, dear, would you like to say a few words on behalf of your husband?"

"Yes, Father," I replied, gripping onto Caden gently for support before heading towards the end of the coffin. "Most of you knew Tony to be a hardened police Lieutenant. I, however, saw him as the man in that picture. Smiling, laughing, and full of life. Who lived life as though the sun would never drop behind the horizon. Tony and I were still learning about one another, creating…" I paused as my hand dropped to the swell of my stomach. "Creating a life I never could have imagined. But one I'd like to build, in his honor, and in his vision. In his vows, he had said, *till death do us part*, but I'm afraid I can't honor that. Because he'll always be with me," I choked, "and our girls."

"Let us pray," Father Layhe replied.

We all bowed our heads in unison.

The service ended with many filtering out, too shy, or awkward to speak to me. The majority of the men in uniform regarding me, telling me stories of Tony that I had yet to learn from him.

"You were one of the best things to have happened to him," Detective Johnson said, squeezing my hands. "Emma, all of you *saved* Tony." I inhaled sharply at that, the crook of my finger catching a stray tear.

This time, there isn't a mysterious stranger lingering in the cemetery. Caden is more than visible, standing between Tony's grave and Nate's. His eyes find me, and they hold me. He opens his arms to collect me after all was said and done.

"Take Grace and wait in the care for me, please?" I asked.

Caden nodded softly, "You sure you'll be alright?"

"I, yeah. I just want to have a moment alone with him," I assured him.

He respected my wishes and took a very sleepy Grace back towards the car. At this point, being so far into my pregnancy, I couldn't kneel. However, I did the next best thing and cupped my swell with both palms. "What will I do without you? What will Grace and Ava-Elizabeth do without you, Tony? I was mad...I was furious that you broke your promise," I hissed a whisper. "But I know you're with Nate and Nina now. You're with God, who'll protect you. Watch over your girls, okay?"

Back at the house, after Grace had been put to bed, I lowered myself at my kitchen table as Caden quickly let Boomer out to do his business before whistling for him to come back inside. By now, Caden knew the ins and outs of my house. I had given him a spare key to come and go for however long he wished to stay with us. He put a kettle on and let the water boil before he came over behind me, and began rubbing my shoulders.

"How are you holding up, Em?"

Did I dare tell the truth? On the inside, I was screaming.

"Tired," I mumbled, but I couldn't deny how good the shoulder rub felt. Leaning forward, my elbows pressed upon the table. I felt the sobs overcome me again. Caden squeezed my shoulders and shook his head, heading back to the kettle just as the steam billowed out from the spout. He wanted to catch it before it could whistle and wake Grace up.

After pouring the hot water into the lemon ginger tea, he carried them over by the handles and set one down in front of me before wrapping his arms around my shoulders once more. "I know, I know," he attempted to comfort me, "It's okay." But that only seemed to make me cry harder.

"No, it's not," I sobbed.

"Can I tell you something?" Though he didn't wait for me to respond. "The night of Tony's death, he came to me in a dream. It was odd, because it was just us in a white space. He stood across from me and told me to tell you that he was alright."

I sniffled, "He did?"

Caden nodded, "Uh-huh. And you know what else he told me? He told me to take care of his girls. He trusted me with the most important women of his life." Caden sunk down into the seat beside me, taking my trembling hand into his before bringing it to his lips and kissing it. "And I told him that he didn't need to ask. I'm here, I'm not going anywhere. I promise you."

Out of all the things at the moment I didn't want to believe, the way Caden was looking at me…how could I not?

Journal...

St. Charles Cemetery all over again. Nate's grave is just in view. I'm losing yet another important person in my life. And while I'm surrounded by so many supportive people, I've never felt more alone....

I'm still angry. I'm seething as I write this, Journal. I don't understand what I've done to have been dealt the hand I've been given. Can someone send me a sign? Something? Anything? Or has what I've done been so terrible to force me to live in this purgatory?

~Emma

Till Death Do Us Part

~Chapter 18~

The New Beginning

"Here's to new beginnings. Cheers!" I said as Caden and I clinked our glasses together.

Caden and I started seeing each other two years after Tony had passed away. He was there when Ava was born five weeks premature and to pick up the pieces when I thought it was possible that I could lose her too.

He slept on my couch for a very long time in the beginning, when I thought I couldn't go on without Tony. He was amazing at juggling taking care of Grace, Ava, and me. Boomer loved him too and I felt sometimes that he thought he was Nate, by the way Boomer acted towards him.

Ava-Elizabeth has always called Caden "Dada," for he is the only father figure she will ever know. Ava-Elizabeth was born with Tony's striking blue eyes, but with the thickest lashes you'd ever find on an infant.

Grace calls Caden, "Kay" and has since she first learned how to speak.

Caden and I have a wonderful relationship, that is slowly blossoming into something serious. He has moved in with us full time and now shares my bed. We finally made love for the first time last night. It was difficult for me to be with another man sexually after being with the man who was the love of my life. I almost feel as though I cheated on Tony.

It has been so hard for me to accept his death, too. I know going forward I will be okay—one day. I see a therapist, who has been so wonderful in helping me to move forward and be the best mother to my girls and a good partner to Caden, as well.

We often speak of the future and getting married. I guess that's up to Caden when he will feel it is the best time. He drops hints and asks me what kind of engagement rings I like. I told him that Tony and I never got engaged. Therefore, I really didn't know what I liked. He laughed and said he'd surprise me one day.

I have decided that staying in the home I bought when I was single and also the same home we stayed in when I married Tony, and got custody of Grace, will always be the home we continue to live in. I do have a lot of wonderful memories in this home. Caden and I have since painted the walls and changed a lot of the furniture to reflect his taste as well as mine. There are pictures that hang above my fireplace of the happier days when Tony was alive, and Nate, too. It has become the gathering place for all our photos. It is also the focal point of our home showing the love of our family.

Sometimes I look at those pictures and feel like I've lived a thousand lives and other times I just see pure love. The road ahead is paved with great beginnings and tons of love that will continue to grow deeper with time.

"Hey Em, did you hear anything I just said?" Laughed Caden.

"Oh my God, no. I'm so sorry, Caden. Say it again."

"Where were you just now, Em?"

"I was lost in my thoughts. Thinking about you, this home, our daughters, and how far we all have come. I love you, Caden, and thank you for always being there for all of us. I don't know how I would have survived without you."

"I love you too, Em. And I will always be by your side if you will have me," Said Caden as he hugged me tightly.

"Yes, of course, I will always be with you, Caden."

"Good, I was hoping you'd say that. Now, Em, I have a very important question to ask you. But first, I need Grace and Ava-Elizabeth to be here with us. Can you please get them?"

"Yes, just give me a minute."

I saw Caden get up and grab the bottle of champagne and our glasses while I went to collect the girls. They were in the next room in the playpen, wearing pink jackets. When did we get them matching pink jackets?

I took Grace and Ava-Elizabeth by the hand and led them into the living room where Caden was pouring the champagne.

"Grace and Ava come stand here next to me. We have to ask Mama an important question."

"Mama?" Said Grace.

"Yes, Mama," laughed Caden. "Em, can you turn the girls around? There's something written on the back of their jackets. I wanted to get your approval."

"You know, I was starting to wonder when we got them. What have you three musketeers been up to?"

"Oh, I made them." He smiled. "Go on, turn them around. I can't wait to see your reaction."

On the front of the jackets were the words: *Pink Babies.* In the similar fashion that the *Pink Ladies* wore on their jackets in *Grease.* Was this a prelude to Halloween? Is that what he was hinting at?

I turned each of them around. On the back of Grace's jacket was the word, *Marry.* I stilled. Nate's smile in Grace beamed at me before I then turned Ava-Elizabeth around. In big, bold stitched lettering was the second half, *Me?*

On top of that, I heard the faint instrumental of a song I undoubtedly recognized coming from Caden's phone. "Hopelessly Devoted to You" was my favorite song, from a film that held such significance to the both of us.

"Caden?" I turned around to find him down upon one knee, holding open a classic velvet box containing a beautiful illusion set diamond in a stunning white gold setting. Very 1950s.

"Em, Grace, Ava-Elizabeth, and I would like to ask you something very important. Will you marry me?"

I was beside myself with joy.

"Oh my God! Yes, of course!" I gushed. "We will now officially be a complete family, isn't that right my baby girls?"

"Mama, Dada!" Both Grace and Ava said at the same time.

I looked down at all three of them and for the first time in a long time, all I saw was my family looking back at me.

DC Caruso

I felt no pain and no hurt for my losses, just pure love for all of them.

Dear Journal,

Through everything I have gone through on this journey, it occurred to me that everything has come full circle. I love Tony. He will always be my first husband, the man of my dreams, the one I never knew I needed in my life until I met him.

But Caden was always there. He has always been a factor in every phase of my life. And perhaps at the time, it wasn't met for us to be where we are now. We're exactly where we're supposed to be, and it makes sense.

I know it's real with Caden. In my own way, I have always loved him.

My life has come together, and in the most perfect way I could have ever imagined.

I want Grace and Ava-Elizabeth to experience a love like this, at least once in their lifetimes. And I know it'll come in varying forms. None of which are wrong. There is no wrong way to love a person, so long as it comes with the right intent.

Tony and I are proof that love can strike at any time.

However, it's Caden and I who show that who is meant to be in your life, no matter where life may take them, will always find a way of coming back.

Ever yours,

Emma

About the author

DC Caruso was born in Bayside, NY, where she fell in love with reading, writing, and romance. She then raised her family of four in Long Island, NY. She is an active participant within her community, is a moderator for a panel of romance writers for the Milford Readers and Writers Festival. She has written six books, thus far. Author DC Caruso currently resides in Pennsylvania with her husband, children, and four legged babies.